ANDREW VACHSS

A Bomb Built in Hell

Andrew Vachss is a lawyer who represents children and youths exclusively. His many works of fiction include the Burke series, several stand-alone novels, and two collections of short stories. His books have been translated into twenty languages, and his work has appeared in *Parade*, *Antaeus*, *Esquire*, *Playboy*, and *The New York Times*, among other publications. He divides his time between his native New York City and the Pacific Northwest.

www.vachss.com

A Bomb Built
in HELL

A Bomb Built in HELL

WESLEY'S STORY

ANDREW VACHSS

VINTAGE CRIME/BLACK LIZARD
Vintage Books
A Division of Random House, Inc.
New York

A VINTAGE CRIME/BLACK LIZARD ORIGINAL,
NOVEMBER 2012

The Library of Congress Cataloging-in-Publication Data
Vachss, Andrew H.
A bomb built in hell : a novel / by Andrew Vachss.
p. cm.
"A Vintage Crime/Black Lizard original."
1. Assassins—Fiction. 2. Ex-convicts—Fiction.
3. Brooklyn (New York, N.Y.)—Fiction. I. Title.
PS3572.A33B66 2012
813'.54—dc23
2012012245

ISBN: 978-0-307-95085-7

www.weeklylizard.com

Printed in the United States of America
10 9 8 7 6 5 4 3 2 1

Victor Chapin died on Sunday, March 6, 1983

John Schaffner Associates, Inc.
425 East 51st Street
New York, N.Y. 10022
MU 8-4763

Jack Van Bibber
391 West Street
New York, N.Y. 10014
WA 4-7839

AUTHOR'S NOTE

In 1972, I was represented by the John Schaffner Agency, largely on the strength of some short stories[1] I published in minor magazines. My first full-length effort was, essentially, the journal I kept during my time in the infamous New York City Welfare Department between 1966 and 1969, ending when I left to enter the war zone inside a country calling itself Biafra.[2] That book was (as was all my work prior to *Flood*) considered unacceptable by the publishing establishment, on the grounds that there was no market for "this kind of material."

---

[1] One of which later morphed into "Placebo," which, still later, came to anchor the three-act play "Replay," both featured in my first short-story collection, *Born Bad* (Vintage, 1994). "Placebo" has been performed in many venues, including the U.K. and Europe.

[2] Neither the country nor the name survived. Nigeria won. The result has been such that no one can be certain that war ever ended.

Victor Chapin, my tireless agent, who never lost faith in me, thought my varied ground-zero experiences (including, by that time, not only the genocidal madness in Africa, but a stint as a federal investigator in sexually transmitted diseases, working as an organizer in Lake County, Indiana, running a center for urban migrants in Chicago, a re-entry joint for ex-cons, and a maximum-security prison for violent youth) would lend themselves perfectly to a "hard-boiled" novel of the type that was so successful in the 1950s. *A Bomb Built in Hell* resulted.

And (again) was unanimously rejected by publishers. They professed to love the writing, but felt the events depicted were a "political horror story" and not remotely realistic. The rejection letters make interesting reading today. Included in the "lack of realism" category were such things as Chinese youth gangs and the fall of Haiti. And, of course, the very idea of someone entering a high school with the intent of destroying every living person inside was just too . . . ludicrous.

Naturally, the book was also "too" hard-boiled, "too" extreme, "too" spare and violent. I heard endlessly about how an anti-hero was acceptable, but Wesley was just "too" much.

Bomb was meant to be a Ph.D. thesis in criminology without the footnotes, exploring such areas as the connection between child abuse and crime, and the desperate need of unbonded, dangerous children to form "families of choice." Thus, the narrative is third-person, and the tone is flat and detached.

Victor, ever loyal, insisted that there was no dispute

about my ability as a writer, but that I needed to add some intimacy to a book everyone called "dry ice." So . . . *Flood*. Same themes, but first-person narrative, interior monologues, fleshed-out backstory, (some) characters with whom the reader could identify (and even, presumably, like). Some sense of human connection. But the same themes.

Victor read the manuscript and told me I had finally done it—we were winners. And then he died. Suddenly and unfairly.

Years later, after *Flood* came out, offers for *Bomb* magically appeared. Some from the same publishers who had rejected it the first time. I never took the offers, thinking of the original book as a "period piece." Later, at the suggestion of Knopf publisher (and my editor) Sonny Mehta, I cannibalized pieces of it for the Burke series. That series took eighteen books to find its own ending, but pieces of *Bomb* made their way into both *Blue Belle* and *Hard Candy*, and Wesley remained a character in the series (despite being "dead" since *Candy*) throughout.

I left *Flood*'s first publisher, Donald I. Fine, for Knopf, and have remained in that new home ever since. Eventually, Vintage assumed publication of all the books in their classic trade paperback form. If you're reading this in print form, it's thanks to Vintage that you are.[3] And for the fact that this is the first professionally edited version of what I wrote so long ago.

---

[3] Vintage maintains *all* of the books from *Flood* on. This has been especially important to me, because people who run across a used or library version of one of the Burke books can, if they choose, read them all in the order written.

Rumors of the original book's existence have been present ever since an excerpt was published in the Harcourt Brace Jovanovich series *A Matter of Crime* about a quarter-century ago.[4]

The rumors are true. And how I wish some of the book's predictions had not proved to be so.

I dedicated *Flood* to Victor Chapin. And I dedicate this to him as well.

It's been a long wait, old friend. I hope it reads as well from where you are now.

Andrew Vachss
New York

---

[4] Volume 4 (1988), edited by Richard Layman and Matthew J. Bruccoli.

A Bomb Built

in HELL

Wesley sat quietly on the roof of the four-story building overlooking the East River near Pike Slip. It was 4:30 on a Wednesday afternoon in August, about eighty-five degrees and still clear-bright. With his back flat against the storage shack on the roof, he was invisible to anyone looking up from the ground. He knew from observation that neither the tourist helicopters nor the police versions ever passed over this area.

In spite of the heat, Wesley wore a soft black felt hat and a dark suit; his hands were covered with dark-gray deerskin gloves. The breeze blew the ash away from his cigarette. Aware of his habit of biting viciously into the filters, he carefully placed the ground-out butt into his leather-lined side pocket before he got to his feet and stepped back inside the shack.

A soft green light glowed briefly as he entered. Wesley picked up a silent telephone receiver and held it to his ear. He said nothing. The disembodied voice on the phone said, "Yes," and a dial tone followed at once. So Mansfield was going to continue his habit: Wednesday night at Yonkers, Thursday afternoon at Aqueduct. It never varied. But he always brought a woman to the Big A, so it would have to be tonight. A woman was another human to worry about, another pair of eyes. It increased the odds, and Wesley didn't gamble.

He walked soundlessly down the steps to the first floor. The building was over a hundred years old, but the stairs didn't creak and the lock on the door was virtually unbreakable. The door itself was lead between two layers of stainless steel, covered with a thin wood veneer.

Wesley stepped into a garage full of commonplace cars. The only exception was a yellow New York City taxicab, complete with overhead lights, numbers, a meter, a medallion, and the "crash-proof" bumpers that city cabbies use so well.

An ancient man was lazily polishing one of the cars, a beige Eldorado that looked new. He looked up as Wesley entered. Wesley pointed to a nondescript 1973 Ford with New York plates.

"Ninety minutes."

"Plates okay?"

"Give me Suffolk County."

Without another word, the old man slipped a massive hydraulic jack under the front of the Ford and started pumping. He had the front end off the ground and the left wheel off before Wesley closed the door behind him.

Wesley took the back staircase to his basement apartment. It was actually two apartments; the wall between them had been broken through so they formed a single large unit. He twisted the doorknob twice to the left and once to the right, then slipped his key into the lock.

A huge Doberman watched him silently as he

entered. Its ears had been completely, amateurishly removed, leaving only holes in the sides of its skull. The big dog moaned softly. It couldn't bark; the same savage who had cut off its ears when it was a pup had cut out its tongue and damaged its larynx in the process. But the Doberman still had perfect hearing, and Wesley didn't need it to bark.

The dog opened its gaping mouth and Wesley put his hand inside. The dog whined softly, as though remembering the emergency surgery Wesley had performed to stop it from choking on its own blood.

Wesley would have killed the human who carved up the dog anyway; dogs weren't the only things that he liked to cut, and a practicing degenerate like that automatically attracted the police, even in this neighborhood.

He had ghosted up behind the target, who was still squatting obliviously before a tiny fire he had built out on the Slip. Wesley sprawled in the weeds, looking like a used-up wino, and quickly screwed the silencer onto a Ruger .22 semi-auto.

The first shot sounded like a soft wet slap, audible for only about fifty feet. It caught the freak in the back of the skull. Wesley stayed prone as he pumped three more bullets into the target's body, working from the mid-spine area upward.

He was about to leave when he heard the moaning. He thought it might have been a little kid—the freak's usual prey—and he was about to fade away when the dog struggled to its feet. Wesley went over then; a dog couldn't identify him.

Wesley still didn't know why he had risked someone spotting him as he quickly cleaned the dog's wounds, protecting his hands against the expected attempts to bite that never came. Or why he carried it back to the old building. It wasn't playing the percentages to do that. But he hadn't regretted it since. A man would have to kill the dog to get into Wesley's place. And that night on the Slip, the Doberman had proved itself very hard to kill.

The police-band radio hummed and crackled as Wesley showered and shaved. He carefully covered his moderate-length haircut with Vaseline jelly; anyone searching for a grip would end up with a handful of grease instead.

Wesley changed into heavy cotton-twill work pants that were slightly too baggy from the waist to the thighs, ankle-length work boots with soft rubber soles, and an off-white sweatshirt with elastic concealed around the waistband. The steel-cased Rolex came off his left wrist, to be replaced by a fancy-faced cheap "aviator" watch. A Marine Corps ring with a red pseudo-ruby stone went on his right hand; a thick gold wedding band encrusted with tiny zircons on his left.

Wesley carefully applied a tattoo decal to his left hand, a tricolor design of an eagle clutching a lightning bolt. The legend "Death Before Dishonor" ran right across the knuckles, facing out. The new tattoo looked too fresh, so Wesley opened a woman's compact that contained soot collected from the building's roof. He rubbed some gently onto his hand until he was satisfied.

Next, he took an ice pick from a steel-drawered tool case and carefully replaced the thick wooden handle with a much slimmer one. The new handle had a sandpaper-roughened surface and a passage the exact size of the ice-pick steel right through its middle. The old steel was anchored to the new handle with a four-inch screw at the top. Wesley applied a drop of Permabond to the screw threads before tightening the new tool.

After laying the ice pick on the countertop, Wesley crossed the room to a brightly lit terrarium which held several tiny frogs. The terrarium was too deep to allow the frogs to jump directly out; still, it was covered with a screen as a precaution.

Four of the frogs were the color of strawberries; the others were green-and-gold little jewels.

Wesley slowly reached in with a tropical-fish net and extracted one of the green-and-gold frogs. He placed the little creature on a Teflon surface that was surrounded by wire mesh. After replacing the cover of the terrarium, Wesley gently prodded the tiny frog until clear drops stood out visibly on its bright skin. Holding the frog down with a forked piece of flexible steel, Wesley rolled the tip of the ice pick directly across the skin of the squirming frog.

He put the ice pick aside, returned the frog to its home, replaced the wire screen across the top, and then dropped the Teflon pan in the steel sink. Holding the ice pick in one hand, he poured boiling water over the Teflon surface so that the residue ran into the drain. He knew, from extensive tests, that the minute secretions of the golden poison-arrow frog were almost instantly fatal. The two men he had tested it on were slated to die anyway, and the buyer hadn't been particular about how they exited.

A circlet of cork was placed around the tip of the ice pick, which was then inserted into the screwdriver pocket of the work pants. Wesley flexed his leg and saw that the outline did not show. He wasn't surprised.

Wesley walked back into the entranceway, where the Doberman now reclined. He didn't bother to see if the dog had food—it knew how to get food or water by pushing one of the levers under the sink. He checked the closed-circuit TV screen above the door, saw that the hallway was empty, and left. The door locked silently behind him.

6:00 p.m. Wesley went up to the garage. The old man was checking tire pressures on the Ford. Wesley noted that the plates had been changed to ones with the characteristic "V" prefix of Suffolk County. He climbed behind the wheel and slipped a key into a slot hidden beneath the dash. An S&W Airweight dropped into his waiting palm. He pushed the release and examined the opened cylinder—three flat-faced aluminum wadcutters and two steel-jacketed slugs—then snapped it closed and put it back under the dash.

He held the pistol in place and turned the key again; the electromagnets regripped and the gun disappeared.

The Ford had four coats of carnauba wax on its dusty-appearing flanks; it wouldn't leave paint smears unless it hit something head-on. Even in the nearly airtight garage, the idling engine was as silent as a tur-bine. Wesley raced the engine, but the volume rose only slightly. He looked questioningly at the old man, who said: "It robs you of some power, but it don't make no noise. If you want to go and you don't care about the sound, just pull the lever next to the hood release."

Wesley pulled the lever. Even with the engine idling, the motor rumbled threateningly.

"Muffler bypass," said the old man.

Wesley drove slowly out of the garage mouth. The street was empty, as it usually was. The old man would have warned him if it were otherwise. He turned onto the FDR Drive, heading for the Triborough Bridge. Traffic was still slow.

The races didn't begin until 8:05 p.m. Of course, Mansfield would be there early, since the Daily Double window opened about 7:25. Wesley hit the exact-change lane on the bridge—one less face to remember him or the car, as unlikely as that was.

Traffic lightened up as he approached Yankee Sta-dium and was moving along fairly quickly by the time he spotted the track ahead on the right. He paid the parking-lot attendant $1.25 and nosed the Ford care-fully along the outer drive of the lot, looking for the spot he wanted. He found a perfect place and pointed the front of the Ford back toward the highway.

Just as he was about to get out, a red-faced atten-dant ran up screaming, "Hey, buddy, you can't park there!"

Wesley computed the risk of arguing and making himself memorable against the gain of having a safe place to exit from. He immediately rejected the idea of a bribe—nobody bribes parking-lot attendants at Yonkers, and any attempt would be remembered. He decided instantly: either he got the spot he wanted, or he'd wait for another night.

The attendant was a fiftyish clown with an authoritarian face. His wife probably kicked him all over the house; but here in the lot he was boss, and didn't want an ignorant working stiff like Wesley to forget it.

"Get that fucking car outta that spot!"

"I'm sorry, sir. I didn't know. I'll do it right now."

Wesley climbed back into the Ford and pressed the ignition-disconnect button with his knee. The starter screamed, but the engine stayed dead. "Shit! Now the fucking thing won't even start!" Wesley made himself sound frightened at the attendant's potential anger, and got the result he wanted: the clown, having established his power, relaxed.

"S'all right, probably just the battery. Maybe it'll start after the races."

"Goddamn! I'll call a garage. But then I'll miss the . . ."

"Oh, hell. Leave it there," the clown magnanimously told him.

And Wesley did. He walked toward the back gate, paid $2.25, got a large token in exchange, slipped it into the turnstile, and passed inside. He paused at a booth that offered "PROGRAMS 75¢" in huge letters across its top. He gave the man three quarters, took the program and a tiny pencil from a cardboard box on the counter, and turned to leave.

The counterman's voice was loud and obnoxious. "Hey, sport, it's a dime for the pencil!"

Wesley never changed expression; he reached in his jacket pocket for another dime and paid the man.

Outside, he moved toward the track, looking for the target. He had plenty of time; Mansfield was a known railbird, and he'd be glued to the finish line before the first race went off. The mob guys usually sat up in the Clubhouse and had flunkies bet for them, but Mansfield liked to see the action up close.

That didn't make things easier for Wesley, just different.

He drifted away from two old ladies on the rail. Experience had taught him that the elderly were the most observant, almost as much as children. At seven-thirty, Wesley went to the $2 Win window and bought five tickets on the Number 5 horse, Iowa Boy. The jerk just in front of him screamed, "The Six horse, ten times," and threw down his hard-earned double sawbuck as though he had just accomplished something major.

Wesley glanced over to the Double window and saw Mansfield just turning away with a stack of tickets in his manicured hands. *Probably wheeled the Double,* Wesley thought to himself, watching to see if anyone else was paying attention.

No point following Mansfield. Wesley went to the men's room. It was filled with the usual winos, misfits, and would-be high rollers, all talking loudly and paying attention to nobody but themselves. Too crowded; he'd have to do the job outside after all.

Wesley had watched Mansfield for three weeks and time was getting short. The target might be leaving for the Coast any day now, and that would end the contract—Wesley would only operate in New York.

Back outside, Wesley saw Mansfield in his usual spot, right against the rail. Iowa Boy was parked out for most of the race but closed like a demon and paid $16.80. From the way Mansfield tore up his tickets and threw them disgustedly into the air, Wesley concluded that the fucking loser was running true to form.

It wasn't really dark enough yet, but Wesley knew that Mansfield always stayed to the bitter end. The fool liked to bet the Big Triple in the ninth race. When he went into the men's room, Wesley followed right behind. But, as he expected, it was impossible to work there.

The crowd kept getting denser and more excited. Wesley hoped for a hotly contested race to really get them all moaning with that sexual roar—the one amateur sociologists mistake for greed—that erupts when the horses come around the paddock turn for the final time.

The seventh race had a few real dogs running—a couple of hopefuls up from Freehold and a couple more on the way down. The tote board showed a possible payoff of almost a grand on a deuce if you coupled the right nags, and the tote board was showing heavy play. Mansfield had gone to the $20 Exacta window, so he'd have something to think about this race for sure.

This kind of work would be easier with a partner, but Wesley didn't work with partners. He had already been down twice, long enough to note that not many men who worked with teams went to prison alone.

Wesley pressed right behind Mansfield, but the target never noticed. He may have been a top professional on his home ground, but at the track Mansfield's nose was wide open—he sold dope, but his jones was strictly for Lady Luck.

The crowd started screaming as soon as the pace car pulled away with the gate, and got louder and louder with every stride. A pacer named E.B. Time was trying to go wire-to-wire at 35–1, and the crowd was berserk—Yonkers was a short-stretch track, and the long shot might actually hold on.

At the paddock turn, the roar swelled and all eyes were glued to the track. The horses thundered down the stretch, with the drivers whipping the shafts of the carts, bouncing up and down, as though the race hadn't been decided in the Clubhouse hours before. Wesley slipped the ice pick from the screwdriver pocket and held it parallel to his right leg, point down.

Five horses hit the wire together as Wesley slammed the poison-tipped ice pick deep into Mansfield's kidney.

The crowd screamed *"Photo!"* as one, straining forward to see the board.

Mansfield slumped against the rail. Only the weight of Wesley's body pressing against him kept him from falling. The ice pick was back in Wesley's pocket a microsecond after doing its work. He backed his way through the crowd unnoticed—they were all waiting on the photo examination for the winner to be posted.

Wesley had already wiped the ice pick and tossed it softly into the grandstand shadows when he heard the first tentative scream. He knew Mansfield had been dead before he hit the ground. The poison on the tip would make sure the sucker had no luck that night. A knife did more tissue damage, but a knife would need more room to make sure it didn't get stuck in the body.

He was out of the gate and shifting the Ford into Drive when he heard the sirens. By that time, thousands of losers were leaving, too, clogging traffic in all directions.

The towel Wesley had previously soaked in kerosene removed the decal tattoo before he was out of the parking lot. He drove the Ford back across the Triborough, discarding the rag out the window, but turned toward Queens instead of Manhattan. Just before the Brooklyn-Queens Expressway, he pulled the car over to the side, where a red Chevy sat with its hood up and no driver in sight. Wesley got out of the Ford, quickly removed his jacket, stuffed both rings and the watch into the pocket, and left it on the front seat.

He reached back in and turned off the Ford's engine, pulling the key out of the ignition. He entered the Chevy, grabbed a new jacket from the front seat, reached in the pocket, and put on the gold Accutron and the sterling ID bracelet he found there. The jacket fit perfectly.

Wesley slammed down the hood of the Chevy and got back inside. The Ford's ignition key started the Chevy immediately, and he pulled it off the shoulder and onto the road. As he glanced back in the rearview mirror, he saw the Ford cutting across traffic to the left-hand lane.

He took the BQE to Roosevelt Avenue and turned right, followed it to Skillman and took that street across Queens Boulevard to the upper roadway of the 59th Street Bridge. Then he crossed the bridge and took Second Avenue all the way to the Lower East Side before he slid into the maze of ugly narrow streets near the Slip.

As he turned onto Water Street, he pushed the horn ring. No sound came from the horn, but the door of the garage opened quickly and quietly, then closed the same way behind him as soon as he was inside.

The old man stood in the shadows, holding a sawed-off shotgun. As soon as he saw Wesley climb out of the car, he put the gun back into its rack. He was already wiping down the Chevy by the time Wesley closed the basement door behind him.

Wesley walked soundlessly down the back stairs, reflexively checking the security systems as he approached his apartment. He reflected ruefully on how much all this protection had cost. The lack of obvious luxury depressed him sometimes, triggering thoughts of the ugly chain of inevitability that had set him up in business for himself.

Seventeen years old and facing a judge for at least the seventh time. Only this time Wesley wasn't a juvenile and couldn't expect another vacation in the upstate sodomy schools. It was the summer of 1952, before heroin was discovered as the governmental solution to gang fighting, and with the Korean War to occupy the attention of the masses.

And it was the same old story—a gang fight, with the broken and bloody losers screaming "assault and robbery" at the top of their punk lungs.

Cops always waited until the fights were over before moving in to pick up the survivors. They arrived with sirens and flashing lights, so that anyone even slightly disposed to physically resist arrest would have more than enough time to get in the wind instead. Wesley had taken a zip-gun slug in the thigh, and couldn't limp off quickly enough.

He was waiting in the sentencing line. The boys had all pleaded guilty; Legal Aid expected nothing less. Wesley was standing next to a stubby black kid who had ended his engagement to a neighborhood girl with a knife. The black kid was in a talkative mood; he'd been this route before, and he wasn't expecting anything but the maximum worst.

"Man, that judge throwin' nickels and dimes like he motherfucking Woolworth's!"

Wesley kept his eyes straight ahead and wondered if there was a way out of the courtroom. But even as his eyes flew around the exits and measured the fat-bellied bailiff, he knew he wouldn't have any place to go but back to the block. Nothing to do there but keep building a sin for himself, as he had been doing ever since he could remember. The State's "training schools" hadn't trained him to do anything but time. Prison was as inevitable in his future as college was for three other defendants he saw waiting: well-dressed young men, accompanied by parents, friends, and lawyers, who were awaiting disposition on a burglary charge. They'd cop probation or a suspended sentence. Wesley wondered why his gang always fought people just like themselves, when it was really privileged weasels like those kids that they all hated.

The Legal Aid lawyer ran over, his chump face all lit up with excitement. *Probably worked a great deal for me to make license plates for twenty years*, thought Wesley, who'd been "represented" by the same firm since he was a little kid. The lawyer grabbed him by the sleeve and motioned him to step over to the side.

"Would you like to beat this rap completely?"

"I already pleaded guilty, man."

"I know that, I know that . . . but the judge is going to throw a Suspended at anyone over seventeen who agrees to join the Army. And you turned seventeen yesterday. So what do you say?"

"How many years would I have to be in the Army?"

"Four years, but—"

"How much time will I cop with this beef?" Wesley interrupted.

"With your record, even with this being your first adult felony, I'd say five to fifteen."

"Sign me up," Wesley told him.

And it went just like that. While the judge was making a fat-cat's stupid speech about the opportunity to serve your country, Wesley was wondering if the Army gave you time off for good behavior. His next stop was a recruiting booth, where they finally removed the handcuffs.

Basic training was at Camp Gordon. Wesley didn't like the heat in Georgia, and he didn't like the loudmouth sergeant, and he didn't like the gung-ho clowns. But it wasn't prison. When his unit got transferred to Fort Bragg for infantry training, conditions didn't improve. But Wesley was already trained to do his own time, and he didn't have anyone to complain to anyway.

He qualified Expert with the M1, the only non-hillbilly to do so. This was immediately noted and praised by the New York contingent, which had already clashed with the Southerners. But the city-breds were too used to fighting each other to mount any kind of sustained drive against a common enemy. So tension was generally discharged in beery brawls, with no one seriously injured.

Wesley stayed away from all that, and hoped like hell he wouldn't get shipped to Korea.

Camp Jackson was right on the northern border, and the scene of many of the war's worst battles. Wesley was assigned there and attached to a special hunter-killer squad. Because he rarely spoke, he was considered stupid and therefore, according to Army standards, highly reliable. He became the team's sniper—again, the only city kid to be so assigned.

The one thing Wesley paid any attention to was his sergeant telling his squad that every time they went out on patrol, the zips were the only thing keeping him from coming back.

The sergeant was a lifer and respected by everyone for his ability to make an excellent living in a lousy situation. But the sergeant didn't realize what a good listener Wesley was, or how concretely he thought.

During a heavy firefight near Quon Ti-Tyen, Wesley's squad was exposed. They all realized they were going down the tubes unless they retreated, and fast. The ROTC lieutenant had already fallen, leaving their sergeant in command. But the sergeant wasn't even thinking about retreat. He kept screaming at his men to advance.

It took Wesley only a piece of a second to realize that it was the *sergeant* who was keeping him from returning to the safety of the base. He pumped four rounds from his M1 into the lifer's back and neck with the same lack of passion that had always produced the best results from his sniper's roost.

Nobody saw the sergeant fall—his was just another body in a whole mess of bodies. Wesley shouted *"Retreat!"* at the top of his lungs. Because he was the last man to pull out, he was later awarded a Bronze Star from his grateful government.

Two months later, Wesley was hit in the leg with a ball bearing from the land mine that had wiped out the three men just ahead of him. Sent down to South Korea for surgery, he made a complete recovery—just in time to take advantage of an R&R in Japan.

Wesley stayed away from the Japanese whores. He couldn't understand how they could feel anything but hate for American soldiers, and he knew what he would do if their positions had been reversed. The crap games didn't interest him, either; gambling never had.

He was sitting quietly in an enlisted men's bar when four drunken Marines came in and started to tear up the place. Wesley slid toward the door. He was trying to get out when he was grabbed by one of the Marines and belted in the mouth. The Marine saw Wesley falling to the floor, and turned his attention back to the general brawl. He never knew Wesley had come off the floor as fast as he went down.

And smashed a glass ashtray into the back of the Marine's neck.

At the court-martial, Wesley couldn't explain how the ashtray had gotten into his hand or why he had reacted so violently to such a minor assault.

The verdict was an Undesirable discharge. But, in consideration of his excellent combat record and that

Bronze Star, Wesley was separated from the service without stockade time added on. Before he was shipped out, Wesley had the chance to visit the Marine in the hospital.

Even paralyzed from the neck down, he caught Wesley's eye across the room. The Marine was lying faceup on a special bed, with tubes running out of his lower body into various bottles and machines. Wesley walked up close until he was sure the Marine could see him. They were alone in the semi-private room; the Marine's roommate was getting physical therapy in the pool.

"You know who I am?" Wesley asked, not sure yet.

"Yeah, I know who you are—you're the man I'm going to kill."

"You? You're a cripple."

"Oh, it won't be *me*, punk. But I'm a Marine, remember? We back each other up, all the way. And once I tell them who—"

Wesley grabbed the pillow from the next bed and held it tightly over the Marine's face. It was strange to see a man struggle with only his neck muscles, but it didn't last long. Wesley replaced the pillow, pulled the Marine's lids down over his bulging eyes, and walked quietly out of the hospital, unnoticed.

The Marine was listed as having suffocated in his sleep. His death was recorded as "combat-related." A medal was awarded posthumously at the ceremony, when he was buried at Arlington with full honors. His family was proud.

Stateside, Wesley took the Army-issue .45 he had smuggled back from Korea and went for a walk late Saturday night. He entered the liquor store on Tenth Avenue off 21st Street and showed the clerk the piece. The clerk knew the routine. He emptied the cash register even as he was kicking the silent alarm into action, but Wesley was out the door with the money before the police arrived.

He found a hotel on 42nd Street near Eighth and checked in with his military duffel, the pistol, and $725 from the holdup. A few hours later, the room's door burst open. Wesley grabbed for his pistol, but the shot that blasted the pillow out from under his face froze him.

On the way out of the hotel, Wesley looked at the desk clerk very carefully. The clerk was used to this; as a professional rat, he was also used to threats of vengeance from everyone who walked past him in handcuffs.

But Wesley didn't say anything at all.

The night-court judge set bail at ten thousand dollars, and asked if he had the money for a bondsman. Wesley said, "I've got around seven hundred dollars," and the arresting officer called him a smart punk and twisted the handcuffs hard behind his back.

Wesley sat in the Tombs for two weeks until his "free" lawyer finally appeared. In what sounded like an instant replay of years ago, the lawyer told him that a guilty plea would get him about ten years behind his record, because the prior felony now counted since he hadn't completed his "commitment" to the military.

Wesley just nodded—a trial was out of the question.

On the way back from the brief talk with his lawyer, Wesley was stopped by four black prisoners who blocked his path.

"Hey, pussy! Where you goin'?"

Wesley didn't answer—he backed quickly against the wall and wished he had his sharpened bedspring with him.

He watched the blacks the way he had watched North Koreans. They were in no hurry—guards never came onto the tier anyway.

"Hey, boy, when you lock in tonight, I goin' to be with you, keep you company. Ain't that nice?"

Wesley didn't move.

"An' if you don't go for that, then we all be in with you. So I don't want no trouble when I come callin', hear?"

They all laughed and turned back to their cells. Wesley walked carefully to his own cell and reached for the sharpened bedspring under his bunk. It was gone.

Every night, the doors to the individual cells were automatically closed by electricity. Wesley just sat and thought about it for a couple of hours, until supper was over. He refused the food when the cart came by his cell and watched the runner smile knowingly at him. That smile convinced Wesley it wouldn't do any good to try and bargain for another shank to replace the one stolen from him.

At eight-thirty, just before the doors were supposed to close, the four men came back. The biggest one, the talker, came forward with a smile.

"Okay, sweetheart, decision time. Just me, or all of us?"

Wesley looked frightened and defeated—he had been practicing in his scrap of mirror for hours.

"Just you," he said, in a shaky voice.

The other three slapped palms with the biggest one, mumbled something about "seconds," and ambled off, laughing. They were about fifty feet down the corridor when the cell doors started to slowly close. Wesley knelt down before the big man. The would-be jockey unzipped his fly and stepped toward Wesley . . . who sprang forward and rammed his head and shoulders like a spear into the bigger man's stomach.

They both slammed backward into the cell wall, and Wesley whipped his knee up, trying to drive it right through the other man's groin into his chest.

The big man shrieked in pain, and slumped forward. Wesley's hands were instantly around his throat, thumbs locking the Adam's apple. Just before the cell doors closed, Wesley stuffed the man's head into the opening, his hands turning chalk-white with the strain.

The three others raced back but were too late; they could only watch as the steel door crushed the big man's skull as easily as if it were cardboard. Their own screams brought the guards, clubs up and ready.

Wesley spent the night in solitary. The special watch assigned reported that he went to sleep promptly at ten-thirty, and slept right on through the night.

Wesley's new lawyer was from the same brotherhood as the others. He ran the usual babble about pleading guilty to a reduced charge, escaping what they always called "the heavier penalties permissible under the statutes."

"This could be Murder One, kid, but I think I can get the DA to—"

"Hold up. How could it be murder *anything*? I didn't plan to waste that motherfucker. I was protecting myself, right?"

"The Law says that if you think about killing someone for even a split second before you do it, you're guilty of premeditated murder."

"If I hadn't killed him, he would have . . ."

"Yeah, I know."

"Sure you do."

Wesley thought it through. He finally concluded that shooting the sergeant in Korea hadn't been premeditated—he didn't remember thinking about it at all, much less for a whole split second. And that Marine had been self-defense—if he hadn't killed him, he was dead meat the minute he was ID'ed.

It was too much to work through right away, so Wesley fell back on the one thing he trusted: waiting. After all, he was going to end up behind bars no matter what, and he knew the jail time would count against State time.

So he refused to plead guilty, and sat for another nine months in the Tombs awaiting trial. Finally, the lawyer came back with an offer to plead guilty to manslaughter in exchange for a suspended sentence, running concurrently, on the armed robbery. He was promised a twelve-year top.

Wesley thought about this. He had a lot of time to think, since he was locked in his cell twenty-three and a half hours a day. They gave the prisoners in the isolation unit showers every two weeks, unless they had a court date, and Wesley always used his daily half-hour to watch and see if the dead man's friends were any more loyal than the Marine's had been.

He reasoned it out as best as he could. Even if he slid on the homicide, he *had* robbed the liquor store; he could sit in the Tombs for another couple of years and still pull major time, so he finally accepted the now-frantic lawyer's offer. The thought of going to trial before a jury was making the poor guy lose a lot of sleep.

The judge asked Wesley, "Were any promises made to you, at this time or at any other time, on which you are relying in your plea of guilty to these charges?" When Wesley answered "Yes," the judge called a recess.

The lawyer patiently explained that statements like Wesley's couldn't be allowed to appear on the transcript. When Wesley asked why that was, the lawyer mumbled something about a "clean record." Wesley didn't get it, and figured he wasn't going to.

After a couple of quick rehearsals, Wesley finally said the magic words, and was rewarded with the promised sentence.

Next stop, Auburn. Wesley spent the required thirty days on Fish Row and hit the New Line together with about forty-five other men. Without friends on the outside, without money in his commissary account, and without any advanced skills in stealing from other prisoners, Wesley resigned himself to doing some cold time. He computed his possible "good time" and reckoned he could be back on the street in six-plus, if he copped a good job inside prison.

He put his chances at about the same as those of copping a good job on the street.

The job he wanted was in the machine shop. It wasn't one of the preferred slots, like the bakery, but the potential for fabricating useful tools made it also a potential for getting his hands on some of the commissary other convicts drew.

Wesley didn't expect anything for free, so he wasn't surprised when the inmate clerk wanted five cartons of cigarettes to get Wesley that assignment. Otherwise, it would be the worst placement possible—making license plates.

He had several offers to lend him the smokes, at the usual three-for-two per week, but he passed, knowing he wasn't ever going to get his hands on anything of value Inside without killing someone first.

So Wesley returned to the clerk's office, expecting to get the plate-shop assignment and preparing to keep a perfectly flat face regardless. But the slip the clerk handed him said "Machine Shop" on top.

"How come I got the shop I wanted?" Wesley asked.

"You bitching about it?" the clerk responded.

"Maybe I am—you said it cost five crates."

"It does. But your ride was paid for."

"By who?"

"Whadda you care?"

"I got something for the guy who paid," Wesley said, quiet-voiced. "You want me to give it to you instead?"

"Carmine Trentoni, that's who paid, wiseass. Now, you got a beef with that, take it to him. I got work to do."

It took Wesley a couple of days to find out who Trentoni was without asking too many questions, and almost another week before he could get close enough to the man to speak without raising his voice.

Trentoni was on the Yard with three of his crew, quietly playing cards and smoking the expensive cigars that the commissary carried at ridiculous prices. Wesley waited until the hand was finished and walked up slowly, his hands open and in front of him.

"Could I speak with you a minute?" he asked.

Trentoni looked up. "Sure, kid, what's on your mind?"

"This: I'm not a kid. Not your kid, not anybody's. I killed a man in the House over that. I haven't got the five crates to pay you back now. If you want to wait for them, okay. If not, you won't see me again."

Trentoni looked dazed; then he looked vicious . . . and then he laughed so hard the tower guard poked his rifle over the wall, as if the barrel could see what was going on and report back to him. The other three men had been silent until Carmine broke up, and then they all joined in. But it was obvious they didn't know what they were supposed to be laughing at.

Carmine got to his feet, a short, heavily built man of about fifty-five, whose once-black hair had turned gray years ago. He motioned to Wesley to follow him along the Wall, away from the game. He deliberately turned his back on the younger man and walked quickly until he was about a hundred feet away from anyone else.

Wesley followed at a distance; he knew nothing ever happened on the Yard unless there was a cover-crowd, but he couldn't understand the laughter, either. Carmine wheeled to face Wesley, his mouth ugly with scorn.

"Punk! Filthy, guttersnipe punk! Raised in garbage, so it's only fucking garbage you understand, huh? Yeah, I sent the five crates to that weasel of a clerk, but what I want from you, *kid*, is nothing! You get that? Carmine Trentoni wants nothing from you and he gave you the five crates for free, no payback. Can your punk mind understand that?"

The vehemence of Trentoni's speech knocked Wesley back, but his habits had been formed years before that day, so he just asked, "Why?"

"Why? I'll tell you why: I know why you're here, which is more than *you* know, right? I know what happened in the House. I laid those five fucking cartons on the clerk because I *wanted* to. And if you try and pay them back, I'll rip the veins outta your punk throat. . . . You got that?"

"Yes."

Wesley turned and walked to his cell, not looking back. It took him another ten days to learn that Carmine was serving three life sentences, running wild, for three separate gang murders, committed more than twenty years ago. He had stood mute at his trial, refusing even to acknowledge the judge or his own attorney. At the sentencing, when asked if he had anything to say for himself, Carmine faced the judge with a pleasant smile.

"You can't kill what I stand for."

He had never elaborated on that statement, not even to the questioning reporters to whom most prisoners were eager to talk. He had never appealed the convictions and had ignored parole hearings for which he was scheduled many years later.

He ran the prison Book, but he wouldn't shark cigarettes or do anything else for money. The rumors were that he had killed twice more while in prison, but nobody really knew who the killer of the two unrelated victims was. They had been found in their cells, one stabbed and one burned to a crisp. There had been no evidence, no witnesses, and no indictments.

Wesley listened until he had heard enough; then he went looking for Carmine Trentoni. He found him standing in a corner of the Yard, watching a couple of his men taking bets. Wesley waited until Carmine's men had finished operating and then walked over. At a silent signal, Carmine's men stepped off to give him room.

"There's something I want to say to you."

Carmine just looked frozen-faced, staring through Wesley to someplace else.

"Thank you for the cigarettes. You're a real man, and I'm sorry for what I thought of you."

Carmine's face broke into a huge grin, and he slapped Wesley heavily on the biceps. "Okay, okay, that's good—I was right about you!"

They shook hands. And from that day on, Wesley went everyplace Carmine did. The first thing Wesley did was quit his job in the machine shop. Carmine had told him:

"What you wanna work in the fucking machine shop for? I'll tell you. One, you think you'll learn something useful for when you're back on the bricks. This is one-hundred-percent wrong, Wes—the only thing you can make in that stinking place is a shank, and you can always buy one. You think they'll let you join the fuck-ing union when you get out? Okay, now, number two, you think you going to impress the Parole Board, right? Wrong—you don't want a fucking parole."

"*Who* don't want a fucking parole?"

"You don't, and I'll tell you why *if* you listen. What you going to do when you get out? You going to work in a gas station, push a garment rack? Gonna wash cars, kiss ass . . . what?"

"I'm going to—"

"*—steal.*"

"Yeah," Wesley acknowledged. "I guess that's what I'll be doing, all right."

"You know why?" Carmine challenged.

Wesley smiled, but it wasn't the icy twisting of his lips that he used on guards. He knew the old man was trying to hand out his last will and testament while he was still alive.

"Why, Pop?"

"Pop! You little punk; I could still kick *your* ass."

"I know you could, old man."

And Carmine realized what Wesley had already learned, and smiled, too.

"*This* is why. Because you a man, a white man, in America, in 1956. And that means you either starve, steal, or kiss ass."

"Is that only for white men, Carmine?"

"No. That is for *any* man. I called you a white man because that's what you are, a white man. But never underestimate any man—humans come in five colors, Wes, and the only color I hate is blue."

"For cops?"

"For cops, and for the kind of feeling you get on Christmas, when you know the only motherfucking way your kids're going to get any presents is if you go out and hit some citizen in the head."

"So why don't I want a parole?"

"Because you gonna steal, kid—and you don't need no faggot parole officer sticking his nose into your face every time you breathe. Come out clean, and then do what you have to do."

"It's a lot more time that way."

"So what? People like us do nothing but time. On the street, in the joint . . . it's all the same. Either place, you can think, you can learn. . . ."

"Like I am now?"

"Yeah, like you are now."

Another year passed. A year of Carmine sharing his income, his stash, his smokes, and his experience. Wesley paid the closest attention, especially to what sounded like contradictions.

He saw the old man smile serenely at the shank-riddled body of what had been a human being carried from the cellblock to the prison morgue. "Now, that's a *nice* way for a rat to check out of this hotel."

But when Carmine told Wesley that his mother must have been Italian because Wesley for sure had some Italian blood, and Wesley told him he didn't know who his mother was, the old man's eyes filled with tears, and he awkwardly put his arm around Wesley's shoulder. A passing con looked at this like he knew something, but the younger man just wrote that con's name on the blackboard in his mind and suffered through the embrace without moving.

"You never underestimate," Carmine told him. "Only buffoons underestimate!"

"What do you mean?"

"That nigger you killed in the House. He never looked in your eyes or he would've looked for another girlfriend. He took it too easy, and he paid hard, right?"

"Right. Why you call him a nigger?"

"He *was* a fucking nigger. And Lee is a black *man*, see? There ain't no words that fit everyone, except rich people—they're all fucking swine."

"Why?"

"Because we want what they got and they don't want to share. Period. That's why you went to Korea, right? To fight their fucking wars."

"Would Lee get hot if he heard you call another guy a nigger?"

"No. Or if he did he wouldn't show it. A man who shows his anger is a fool, and fools don't live long. Revenge is dessert. First you eat the meal, no matter how fucking bad it tastes. Always, *always* remember that. Your patience is always one second longer than your enemy thinks it is."

"What are you waiting for now?" Wesley asked.

"Just to die, kid. There's nothing out there for me. In here, those people take care of my family, and after I go they'll keep doing it. I'm going to die the way I lived: with a closed mouth. Those people appreciate that— they *have* to. But if I was to go out there, they'd expect things of me that I won't do anymore."

"Like what?"

"To respect them."

"You don't. . . ?"

"Not no more. Our thing is dead, Wes—it's dead and fucking buried. There's no organization, no mob, no fucking *Mafia* or whatever the asshole reporters want to call it. It used to be a blood thing, but now it's just criminals, like the Jews used to be."

"*Jews* used to be big criminals?"

"Kid, they was the *worst.* Used to be you couldn't be in crime in New York unless you was Jewish. The Irish came after them, and then we came after the Irish. And now it's time to bury us, too."

"Who's next?"

"The blacks, the Latins . . . who knows? Maybe the fucking Chinese. But it'll all end the same. Greedy, stupid bastards."

"Then I couldn't . . ."

"No, kid, there's no place for you. Even if I recommended you, you'd just be a soldier in someone's fucked-up army. But I've been thinking a long time. And before I check out of here, I'll tell you what you *can* do."

The next two years went by unchanged. Carmine ran the Book as he always did—on the square—and his customers were never lured away by promises of bigger payoffs elsewhere. Too often, those bigger payoffs were a shank planted in some sucker's chest. Besides, Carmine was the old, established firm, and prisoners are a conservative lot.

Dayton was trouble from the day he hit the Yard. A tall, over-muscled motorcycle freak, he gorilla'ed off a couple of young kids easily enough. This immediately gave him some highly inflated ideas about prison reality. The older cons just shook their heads and predicted a quick death for him, but Dayton stayed alive through his combination of strength, skill, and stupidity.

But the only part of that combination that grew was stupidity. He bet fifty packs with Carmine on the Yankees in the 1960 Series. He lost. And when he passed

Carmine and Wesley on the Yard the next day, he strolled over to them.

"You looking for your fifty packs, old man?"

"Do I *have* to look for them?"

"Nah. Don't look for them. Because I'll cut your throat first."

Wesley stayed relaxed—he heard this kind of bullshit threat every day on the Yard, and Carmine could handle the ticket-sellers in his sleep. But before he turned his head away, Dayton leaned over Carmine, whispered, "And just so you know . . . ," and slapped him viciously across the face.

The next thing Wesley remembered was the hack's club smashing into the back of his head for the third time. He woke up in the hospital. When he opened his eyes, he saw Carmine staring down at him.

"You okay, kid?" the old man asked.

"Yeah. Is he dead?"

"He will be in about an hour."

"I didn't kill him?"

"No, thank the Devil, you didn't."

"I will as soon as I get out of here."

"Be too late then, you stupid punk!"

"What . . . Why'd you say that, Pop? I did it for you."

"The *fuck* you did. You did it for *you*, right? You couldn't stand the profile of being partners with the kind of old man who'd take a slap in the face from a buffoon. So you try to snuff him right on the Yard. Stupid . . . stupid fucking kid."

"Listen, Carmine, I—"

"No, *you* listen, Wesley. You *never* lose your temper, or someday you lose your head. Now, this is only a minor beef you got—fighting on the Yard, no weapons, no sneaking up, and the other guy's not dead. You gonna get thirty days in the Hole behind it and a black tab on your jacket, but so what? If you'd taken him off like you tried to, you never get outta here . . . never."

"So what?"

"So what? Don't be a fucking *cafone*, so what! You got a lot to do."

"What?"

"I'll tell you when you get outta the Hole. And while you're there, be thinking about this: that cocksucker was twice as big as you, but you almost dropped him anyway, because you jumped him in hot anger. If you took him in his sleep with *cold* anger, what you think would have happened?"

The thirty days in the box were actually a relaxed time for Wesley. Carmine had books and cigarettes smuggled in by the runners. And the guards transmitted the daily messages. Carmine's notes were always instructions.

> *practice not moving a muscle until you can do it for all the time between meals*
> *practice breathing so shallow your chest don't move*
> *think about the person you hate most in the world and smile*
> *the head plans the hands kill the heart only pumps blood*

Wesley read each note until he was certain he had it memorized, then burned it and flushed it down the lidless toilet.

When he was released, Carmine was waiting for him. The old man's juice had kept his cell unoccupied during his absence.

"What'll I do now?" Wesley asked.

"Right now?"

"When I get out."

"Damn, kid, didn't you think about nothing else all the time you were down?"

"Yeah, everything you wrote me."

"Can you do it?"

"Just about."

"That's not good enough. You got to get it perfect."

"Why am I learning all this?"

"For your career."

"Which is?"

"Killing people."

"Which people?"

"Look, Wes, how many men you already killed?"

"Three, I guess." Wesley told him about the sergeant and the Marine, all the time wondering how Carmine knew it was more than one.

"How many felony convictions you got?"

"A few, I guess. There's this beef, which was really two, and a couple before when I was a juvenile, and the Army thing . . . I don't even know."

"You know what 'The Bitch' is?"

"No."

"Habitual Offender. In this state you get three felony drops and they make you out to be 'dangerous to society'—it's a guaranteed Life for the third pop. Understand what I'm telling you, Wes? The next time you fall, you fall forever. Whether it's a lousy C-note stickup or a dozen homicides, you get the Book. And killing people pays a lot more than sticking up liquor stores."

"What about banks?"

"Forget it. You got the fucking cameras taking your picture, you got the fucking *federales* on your case for life, and you got to work with partners."

"That's no good?"

"How many partners you got?"

"Just you."

"That's as far as you can go, but I won't ever make the bricks. You'll have a partner again, but make me the last person you ever trust with *all* your business. You gonna meet all kinds of people, but don't ever let anyone see your heart or your head. Just your hands, and only if they make you do it."

"How do I do this?"

"I'll give you the names to get started: who to contact, how to do it without getting into a cross. After a couple of jobs, you'll have all the work you want."

"What're the rules?"

"You can say 'yes' and you can say 'no.' But—you say 'yes,' you got to get it done, whatever it costs. And if you fall, you say nothing . . . no matter what. That's all."

"What else, Pop?"

"Cold: you got to be cold right on through. And you got to show me you *are* that cold before we go any further with this."

"I am. I am right now."

"Yeah? Okay, then. Listen, because we don't got a lot of time. Dayton's already been done, but he had a partner. Another stupid animal. He wants me, and he thinks he's being slick by waiting for a shot, okay? His name's Logan, and he locks in Seven-Up. Ice him—and don't let me even *guess* how you did it."

Carmine started talking about the football-season betting, telling Wesley that the subject was dropped. And that he'd have to pick it up himself if he wanted to continue the conversation. Ever.

It took Wesley five weeks to learn that Logan was a Milky Way freak. Another three to get the hypodermic needle and syringe from the prison hospital. Two weeks more to steal a pinch of rat poison from the maintenance crew.

Just buying would have been quicker—all of those items were for sale Inside—but he understood Carmine expected him to act without leaving a trail. The only way to get that done was to act completely alone.

The real risk was getting into the commissary area without being seen, and pure patience solved that problem. Wesley took all but four of the Milky Ways. He carefully injected what he left behind with a mixture of strychnine and water, then painstakingly smoothed over the tiny holes the needle left in the dark wrappers.

The next morning, as he turned away from the commissary window, Wesley walked past Logan, who was only a couple of men behind him. Wesley muttered, "No more fucking Milky Ways for two weeks."

At 4:05 a.m., the whole tier woke up to Logan's screaming. By the time the hacks got there with the inmate nurse, he was already turning blue. They rushed him off to the hospital on a stretcher.

Logan held on through the night and even rallied slightly the next day. The poisoning had not been discovered, because the greedy sucker had eaten his entire supply before going to sleep. It was too late to pump his stomach. And they wouldn't waste State money on an autopsy.

Wesley walked by the hospital a dozen times that day, but it was never empty enough. Just before supper line, he slipped inside and saw that the guard was in the bathroom, probably moving his lips as he read a porno magazine piously confiscated from a convict. Wesley pulled the crude, needle-pointed file from under his shirt and wrapped the handle in a rag pulled from his belt. Logan never looked up at Wesley's soundless approach. He grunted as the spike slammed into the left side of his chest, right up to the hilt. Reflexively, his hands grabbed at the file's handle.

One look told Wesley that Logan was gone. With his own fingerprints all over the murder weapon.

Wesley caught the supper line near the end, picked up his tray, and sat down at his usual place with Carmine. He deliberately looked down into the pseudo-chicken and mashed potatoes until Carmine followed his gaze.

Wesley drew an "X" across the top of the mashed potatoes with his fork. The old man grunted in acknowledgment.

The word was down the grapevine by the time they returned to the block for lockup after supper. The rec room buzzed with the news, but that was soon replaced by an almost homicidal argument over which TV show to watch. Wesley and Carmine faded back toward the rear of the large room.

"You crazy fuck. Why'd you stick him?"

"He was going to get better."

"Clean?"

"*His* prints are the only ones they'll find."

"Why'd you only fix a couple of the bars?"

"Didn't want anybody else to get it. He was at the end of the line. I knew he'd buy up all four left if anyone else got there first."

"That's half smart, kid. Sometimes, you can be *too* slick. If you'd done every bar in the place, you wouldn't need to steal any. And there would've been no way for that fucking swine to get off the hook."

"Sure, but if more than one guy went, they'd do a big investigation, right?"

"So what? What do they find? Nothing about you. And why'd you give him such a light dose that he could get up behind it?"

"I didn't know how much to use."

"Then you shouldn't have used that stuff at all."

"It was all I had."

"No, Wes—you had the library."

"The *library*?"

"There's a lot of things in books they never meant us to know, you understand me?"

"Like what you said about the history books—that the winners write the stories after they win the wars?"

"Not just that—I'm talking about facts. Like how you make a bomb, what's inside of a poison, how you fix guns, how much money a politician makes, what the fucking laws say . . ."

"There's things you can't learn from books."

"Sure. Now you talking like a real chump. What 'things'? *You* learning these things, kid?"

"In here? Sure."

"You ever listen to Lester when he talks?"

"That fucking skinner. Who'd listen to that disgusting little piece of shit?"

"You would, if you had any sense. You think you'll never be tracking a man in Times Square? You think people like Lester ain't all over the place there? If you going to run in the jungle, you'd better know *all* the animals."

"How come you don't study him, then?"

"I *have* studied him, Wes. But I don't get too close, because I have to live in here the rest of my life. I can't let anyone think I'm changing my game after all these years. That's what gives them ideas. But if I was going out, I wouldn't just be studying Lester, I'd be studying every freak, every maniac, every sick-ass in this joint, until I knew exactly what makes them run. And I'd use it on the street. Why you think the shrinks are always studying Lester? Anything the big bosses want to know, you got to figure is worth knowing, too, right?"

"How do I make him talk?"

"You don't need to *make* him talk. Just forget your fucking image and listen—he'll do all the talking you'll ever want."

"What about Logan?"

"Who's that?"

Another long year passed. Wesley divided his time between the library, the cellblocks, and the Yard. Always listening and learning. Part of that was learning to say nothing, except when forced.

But he spent as much time as possible with Carmine, because the old man was obviously hanging on by a fine thread, even if his reputation kept anyone from sawing at it.

One dirty, gray morning, the Yard was nearly empty. Carmine had told Wesley to meet him at their spot by eight-thirty. Wesley had arrived early, and stood motionless in the shadows, as he had been taught. Finally, he recognized the old man's bulk as it rounded the corner.

"Morning, Pop."

"I got no more time, Wes. Listen to me as good as you ever did, and don't say a word until I'm done. I'm checking out of here. Maybe this morning, maybe tonight . . ."

"You're not—"

"*The fuck'd I just tell you?*" the old man hissed in a whisper. "Shut up and listen: I made out my will, and you're the beneficiary. Sit down with me here against the wall."

The two men hunkered down against the wall, ignoring the dampness. Wesley went stone-cold quiet, because one sidelong glance told him the old man wasn't going to get up again.

"You got to *remember* all this, Wes—you can't be writing it down. When you wrap up, you go to Cleveland; that's in Ohio. Take the bus in, but fly out, understand? Don't use the big airport going back, the one they call Hopkins. They got a little commuter airport in Cleveland. Like for businessmen, so be sure you got a suit on. Israel, he'll fix you up with that.

"Anyway, if the wheels come off, remember you want Burke Airport. It's right on the lake—just tell any cabbie to take you; they'll know.

"Okay, now, when you get to the bus station in Cleveland, you go to the King Hotel, that's at Fifty-fifth and Central. You make sure you go there between midnight and two in the morning. Tell the desk clerk you got a message for Israel."

"Like the country?"

"Yeah, like the country—but Israel is a man, a black man. You tell him you're Carmine's son and you're there to pick up what he left. You say that, and Israel, he'll give you the name of someone to hit. And on this one you can't say 'no,' you understand? You can't say 'no.'"

"I won't."

"Okay. After the hit, Israel is going to give you a package. You take what's in there and go back to New York. You go to Mamma Lucci's—it's a restaurant near the corner of Prince and Sullivan, just north of Houston. You ask to speak to Mr. Petraglia, okay?

"You tell *him* you're Carmine's son, same as you told Israel. You give him the package Israel gave you. Then he'll know who you are for sure. This man, he'll show you a building to buy."

"How am I going to—?"

"You'll *have* the money. After you buy the building, you fix it up the way it needs to be. Pet's gonna live there, too. He's the last of us, kid, and one of the best. He can do things with cars you wouldn't believe. But he's not going with you on jobs. At least, not too close."

"But . . . what if Israel's dead when I get there? Or Mr. Petraglia?"

"You got two years, four months, and eleven days to serve out. They'll both live that long. They been waiting for you—they won't leave before you show."

"But if—"

"*If* Israel is gone, go back to New York and call my wife at that number I gave you. Tell her Carmine said to get out of the house. Take a *vacation* for a couple of weeks and tell you where she'll leave you the key. Make sure you say 'vacation.'

"In the basement, the fourth beam from the door holding up the ceiling is hollow in the middle. Cut it down. There's fifty thousand dollars in clean bills there. Take it, and go see Petraglia, tell him what you had to do. But if Israel is in Cleveland, don't call my wife. She has her own money coming, you understand? The basement, that's your case money—it's safer there than anyplace you could find on your own."

"What's case money?"

"Just *in* case. Get it?"

"Yeah."

"All right, there's just one more thing. You know why you're going to do all this?"

"I know why, Pop."

"Who taught you why?"

"You did."

"That makes you my blood, understand? And my blood's gonna keep on flowing even after they all think they're safe. I'm going out, but you're going to pay back every last one of those traitors for me."

"I will."

"I know. I waited years for you to come. Remember I told that judge that they couldn't kill what I stood for? Well, this is perfect revenge. They buried me in hell, all right. But I built a bomb right down here, and it's going to blow their yellow hearts right out of their chests."

"I'll see you soon, Carmine."

"I guess you will, son. But make it count for something while you're out there."

"Pop, was I the best of the lot? Or was it that you couldn't wait any longer?"

"No! You were the one I *wanted*. You are my *son*. I could have waited a hundred more years. . . ."

Carmine's last words trailed off as he slumped back against the Wall.

Wesley walked away. Even though he was known to be the old man's partner, he was never a suspect. There wasn't a mark on the old man, and the autopsy showed a massive aortic aneurysm. The only thing that confused the doctors was that the burst vessels showed that the old man had been dead for more than an hour when the guards found him. But medicine is an imperfect science, and prisons don't pay for medical investigations, anyway.

The hack strolled down the tier to Wesley's cell, carrying a piece of paper in his hand and a concerned look on his fat face.

"Listen, kid—you want to go to the old man's funeral?"

"Yes, sir, I really would. Could you fix it so that I could?"

"Well, I *might* be able to if we could really talk, you know?"

"No, sir, but I'll talk with you about anything you want to know."

"Good," the guard said, walking into Wesley's cell and lowering his voice. "The old bastard left some money stashed, right?"

"I don't know, sir. Did he?"

"That's the way you want to play it, you're out of luck. Let the fucking rats be his pallbearers."

Wesley just looked blankly at the guard, thinking, *That's what he'll have, anyway.* He kept looking straight ahead until the guard finally left in disgust. Wesley had already checked the law and knew he wouldn't be allowed to attend a funeral—he wasn't a blood relative in any sense recognized by the State.

When he hit the Yard almost three weeks later, a slender Latin guy was running the Book, and Carmine's stash of cigarette cartons under the loose floorboards in the back of the print shop was all gone.

Wesley passed by the Latino without a glance. He wrote off the cigarettes and the Book. Even the whispers about a man being a pussy if he wouldn't fight for what was rightfully his.

He did the next years like moving through cold, clear Jell-O. He was able to dodge parole twice by infractions of institutional rules. But the last time, when he only had nine months to go on his sentence, he knew that they were going to parole him to keep him under supervision, no matter what he did. He knew a hundred ways to fuck up the parole hearing, but he didn't want the additional surveillance that came with getting a "political" label, and he didn't want the additional time that an assault would add on. So he spent several respectful hours talking with Lee until he learned what the older man knew.

Wesley appeared before the Board unshaven and smoking a cigarette. The Chairman, some kind of reverend, spoke first.

"Is there any reason why we should parole you at this time?"

Wesley broke into sincere and hearty laughter.

"What is so funny?"

"Man, you *got* to parole me—I'm nine months short."

"That doesn't mean anything to us. We want to know what you've done to rehabilitate yourself."

"I haven't done one motherfucking thing. But so what? You guys *always* parole a man who's less than a year short—that's the law, right? Besides, I did all this time for nothing. I'm innocent."

"That's not the law!" the reverend proclaimed self-righteously. "Your case will be reviewed like any other."

"But the guys in the block said . . ."

"Oh, so *that's* it. Who're you going to listen to, this Board or a bunch of prisoners?"

"But I thought . . ."

"Now, we may parole you *anyway*, but you shouldn't listen to—"

"See! I knew you were just kidding me, man."

"This hearing is concluded. Return to your unit!"

The note from the Board said he was being denied parole due to his "poor institutional adjustment."

They kicked Wesley loose on a Tuesday. He was among eight men going home that day, but the only one who wasn't being paroled. He noticed one guy already nodding from his morning fix and wondered if the pathetic sucker would find the stuff as easy to score on the street as he had Inside.

The State provided a suit, twenty-five dollars, and transportation to the Port Authority Terminal in Manhattan. The factory-reject suit screamed *PRISONER!* as loudly as black and white stripes would have, and Wesley's dead-white face ensured that that impression would register with any cop who bothered to look.

But nobody was looking. Wesley saw at once why Carmine had told him to learn from Lester—the terminal was a swirling river of predators and prey.

He thought about trying to get some fresh clothes,

but he knew Israel wouldn't care what he looked like. And he wasn't going to leave the terminal, anyway.

The Greyhound to Cleveland cost $18.75. Fifteen hours later, Wesley grabbed a cab in Public Square, and he was standing in front of the King Hotel just before midnight. He watched the whores shriek to passing cars for another fifteen minutes before he went inside and walked up to the desk clerk.

"I've got a message for Israel."

"He not here, man."

"I'll wait."

The clerk tried a hard look for a few seconds. Then he dropped his eyes and went out a back door. Ten minutes later, a husky man with a blue-black face and a full beard came down the stairs.

"I'm Israel," the man said. "Come on up to my room."

They walked upstairs to Number 407 and went inside. The man motioned Wesley to a chair near the window and pulled a short-barreled pistol from his inside pocket in the same motion. The gun was only vaguely pointed in Wesley's direction, but his eyes were locked into Wesley's face.

"What are you here for?"

"I'm Carmine's son."

"And . . ."

"I'm here to pick up what he left."

"You know what that is?"

"He said Israel would show me."

"He tell you anything else?"

"That I'd be doing a job of work for you."

"You know who?"

"No."

"You care?"

"No."

"If you're Carmine's son, you must know the only color he hates."

"A cop."

"Yeah, a cop. A pig-slob maggot of a motherfucking cop. He—"

"I don't care what he did. You going to get me everything I need?"

"Which is?"

"A place to stay, some correct clothing, a street map of this town, some folding money to get around with, a couple of good pieces, some tools, some information."

"I can get all that. Shit, I *got* all that already."

"Okay. Show me where I can sleep."

"You want me to drive the car?"

"What car?"

"He's a foot patrolman—that's about the only way you'll get a shot at him."

"I work by myself. I'll think of something."

It took Israel only until the next morning to come up with everything he'd been asked for. Wesley spent an entire day trying to fashion a silencer for the .357 Magnum, and then he decided he couldn't take a chance with a homemade job and unscrewed the tube with regret. He knew you could only silence a revolver but so much anyway.

The pistol was a Colt Python. Wesley dry-fired hundreds of times before he got the hang of making the piece repeat quickly enough. It reminded him of how the Army taught him to use a .45. They made him drop the hammer endlessly with a pencil jammed down the barrel, so the eraser cushioned the firing pin. After a short while, it felt natural.

The target patrolled Central Avenue four-to-midnights; his route took him right by the front door of the hotel. Wesley managed to get up on the roof of the tallest building across from the King, but it only took him a few seconds to write that option off. The lighting on the street was lousy. And the cop always walked with a partner—he'd never be able to tell them apart at that distance.

So he went back to Israel and told him he needed two things: a good double-barreled shotgun—a .12 gauge that could handle three-inch shells—and a telephone call.

Thursday night. Wesley had been waiting in the hotel for four weeks without going outside once. The patrolman and his partner turned off Euclid and started walking up Central toward 55th. Israel came up to Wesley's room and knocked softly.

"They'll be out front in five to ten minutes."

"Be sure to sound like a real nigger on the phone."

"Don't worry about a thing, man—I *am* a real nigger."

Israel picked up the phone and deliberately dialed the police emergency number. When the Central Exchange answered, the operator heard: "Lawd have mercy!

Po-leece! Dem niggahs got dat nice officer an' his friend bleedin' in da street! They gonna kill 'em—they all crazy! You got to . . . What? Right next to dat Black Muslim place on Superior. Dey gonna . . . No, ah *cain't* hang on, ah got to . . ."

Israel rang off just as Wesley passed by his door with the shotgun under a brown raincoat. The gun fit comfortably, now that the barrels had been sawed off down to fourteen inches.

The two officers walked by the front entrance to the hotel, past the winos and the junkies and the hustlers and the whores and the idlers and the vermin. Mr. Murphy, Mr. and Mrs. Badger, and Miss Thing . . . all waiting on Mr. Green. Business as usual.

Wesley stepped out of the doorway, brought up the shotgun, and pulled the wired-together triggers simultaneously. Both cops were blown backward against a parked car. Wesley had two shots from the Colt into each of them before the sea of don't-want-no-Law-on-*me* people could even start to disappear. He didn't know which cop was his target, so he walked over to what was left of them and placed the barrel of the pistol against the right eye of one and pulled the trigger. The back of the cop's head went flying out in a swirling disc of bloody bone. Wesley repeated the work on the other one, and quickly stepped back into the hotel lobby. The lobby was empty—even the desk clerk was gone.

As he walked calmly up the stairs, Wesley wiped down the guns with a black silk handkerchief. He left them on the bed in his room, picked up the nine-by-twelve manila envelope lying there, and stuffed it deep into his belt, all the way to the base of his spine.

Then he grabbed the waiting airline bag and climbed out the window. The fire escape took him to the roof, within six feet of the next building. He leaped lightly across and took the next fire escape down the other side, into the shadows on 55th.

He got into the back of a parked cab whose lights immediately went on.

As the cab motored serenely toward Burke Airport, Wesley noted with satisfaction that the meter already read $3.10, just in case.

The private plane touched down at LaGuardia. Wesley walked across the huge parking lot and kept moving all the way to Roosevelt Avenue in Queens. It took him more than an hour, but he wasn't in a hurry. He grabbed an IRT Elevated on Roosevelt and changed at 74th Street for an E train, which took him right into the Port Authority. He lit a cigarette with the airline ticket stub and checked his pocket for the stub he had picked up from the cabdriver in Cleveland—half of a round-trip bus ticket between Port Authority and Atlanta, Georgia.

Inside Port Authority, he bought a copy of the *Daily News*, drank some prison-tasting orange juice, and watched the degenerates parade until it was almost ten in the morning. Then he took a cab uptown to 60th Street and, with the expensive leather suitcase he had purchased and carefully scuffed up, checked into the Hotel Pierre. He was not asked to pay in advance; the suit Israel had picked out for him in Cleveland easily passed muster.

In the hotel bathroom, he examined the envelope for the first time. It held two hundred and twenty thousand dollars in hundreds. The tightly packed bills looked used, and the serial numbers were not sequential.

Wesley settled his bill at the Pierre. They never even glanced at the hundred-dollar notes. The hotel was far more expensive than others he could have used, but the guidebook he'd read in prison told him the Pierre wasn't the kind of joint where the night clerk would be on a police payroll.

He took a cab to the corner of Houston and Sixth, paid the driver, and threw a half-buck tip. Then he walked north until he saw the cab circle back and re-enter traffic, after which he turned around and headed for Mamma Lucci's.

It was four-fifteen in the afternoon, but the restaurant was evening-dark. Wesley didn't know what Petraglia looked like, except that he'd be old. He walked to a table, deliberately selecting a seat with his back to the door. Wesley ordered spaghetti and veal cutlet *milanese* and asked the waiter if Mr. Petraglia was there yet.

"Who wants to know?"

"I do."

"So? What're you, a cop?"

"I'm from the Board of Health."

The waiter laughed and left the table. In about ten minutes, an ancient old man sat down silently across from Wesley. His voice was so soft Wesley had to lean forward to catch all of the words.

"Who're you related to that I know?"

"To Carmine. I'm his son."

"So! How do I know this?"

"Put your hand under the table."

Wesley slipped the envelope he had picked up in Cleveland into the old man's hard, dry hand.

"Take that someplace and open it up," he told the older man. "Carmine said you'd show me a building to buy."

The old man left the table. He returned within a minute.

"If you hadn't brought it back here, I never would have known. Carmine never said anything to me, never described you, nothing. You could've left the country with that much cash. Carmine told me his son would come here one day. With money—that exact amount. But he told me all this before they took him away the last time. I didn't know what you'd look like or when you'd be coming."

"But you knew I'd come?"

"Yes. This means Carmine's dead?"

"They buried his body."

"I understand. You come with me now. I got to set you up until we can get the building."

The old man's car was a dusty black 1959 Ford with a taut ride. He drove professionally, whipping through traffic without giving the appearance of going fast.

"We'll talk in the car. Nobody hears then, okay?"

"Whatever you say."

"I got the building all picked out. It's on the Slip. . . . You know where that is?"

"Over far east, by the river?"

"Yeah. It used to be a shirt factory, but now it's dead-empty. We can get it for less than half of this money and use most of the rest to fix it up right."

"I'm going to live there?"

"You and me, too, son."

"My name's Wesley."

"Pet—my family call me Pet."

"Carmine said Mr. Petraglia."

"That was so I could make the decision first, get it? You call me Pet. What if you got to call me in a hurry— you gonna say all them syllables?" The old man laughed high up in his dry throat. Wesley nodded in agreement.

Petraglia took him to a house in Brooklyn. Its garage led directly into the basement, which was double-locked from the outside.

"You stay here. Maybe three weeks, maybe a month. Then we'll be ready to move into the building. There's a john in the back, plenty of food in the refrigerator, got a TV and a radio. But only play them with the earplugs— nobody knows you're down here, right?"

"Okay."

"You're not worried that it might take so long?"

"I been waiting a lot longer than that."

"I figured you had to be Inside with Carmine. We got to do something about that paleface shit—a cop would make you in a second. There's a sunlamp down here, too, and some lotion."

"Will the people upstairs hear the toilet flush?"

"Just me is upstairs and I don't hear a thing. I'm not really worried about anybody seeing you—I'd just prefer it, you know? You got a PO to report to?"

"Just you, Pet."

The old man smiled and went out, leaving Wesley alone. Wesley dialed his mind back to solitary confinement and did the next nineteen days in complete silence. He kept the radio on and the earplugs in most of the time, listening to the news with careful attention. He watched the TV with the sound off and looked carefully at the styles of clothing, haircuts, and cars; the way people carried themselves. He familiarized himself with how the Yankees were doing and who was mayor and everything else he could think of, since there was no library in Pet's basement.

There was no telephone, either. Wesley didn't miss one.

When Petraglia returned to the basement, he found Wesley totally absorbed in the TV's silent screen, lying perfectly motionless on the floor in what looked like an impossibly uncomfortable position. The old man motioned Wesley to turn the set off, ignoring the pistol which had materialized in the younger man's hand when he entered the door.

"How in hell can you lay on the floor like that?"

"I can do it for at least three hours," Wesley assured him.

"How d'you know that?"

"I already did it yesterday. And I found the piece in the toilet tank." The old man seemed to understand both Wesley's gymnastics and his search of the premises and said nothing more about it.

They got back into the Ford and drove all the way out to the old shirt factory. It was dark on the FDR, and pure pitch-black once they turned into the Slip. Every streetlight in the neighborhood seemed to be smashed. The old man pressed the horn ring, but no sound came out—the side of a filthy wall seemed to open up, and he drove inside almost without slowing down. Another press on the horn ring and the same door closed silently behind them.

"This here is the first floor. We'll use it like a garage, since it used to be a loading bay. You going to live just below this. The rest of the place is empty, and it's like a damn echo chamber. I got the whole place mined—I'll show you the schematic before we go upstairs—enough stuff to put this building into orbit. We got a phone in the electrical shack on the roof."

"What's an electrical shack? And what if someone hears it ring?"

"The shack is where they used to keep the compressors and the generators for the factory before they closed this place. And the phone *don't* ring. It don't work until you alligator-clip the receiver. I know what I'm doing, Wesley." The old man sounded mildly hurt.

"I know that. Carmine said you were the best."

"*One* of the best is what Carmine would have said, but he didn't know what was happening out here. The rest are gone, and now I *am* the best."

Wesley smiled and, after a second, the old man smiled, too. They walked down the stairs to the apartment Pet had fixed up for him, Pet showing the security systems to Wesley as they walked. The walls on the lower level were all soundproofed, but Pet still kept his voice prison-soft as he talked.

"I'll have a job for you soon. Now, remember, there are a couple of rules in this kind of work: One, you never hit a man in his own home or in front of his children. Two, you never hit a man in a house of worship. Three, you *only* hit the man himself, nobody else."

"Whose rules are these?"

"These are the rules of the people who make the rules."

"Then they don't mean nothing—I'm coming for them, too."

"I know that. I know what Carmine wanted. I'm just telling you so's you know how to act in front of them if that ever happens."

"What you mean, in front of them?"

"You never know, right?"

"Them, too?"

"I mean, they're the real ones, right? Rich people?"

"Yeah, rich people . . . *very* fucking rich people, Wesley."

"Good. Now show me the rest."

It took another ninety days for the place to fill up completely to Pet's satisfaction. The generator he installed would enable the place to run its electrical systems without city power. The freezer held enough for six months, and the old man installed a five-hundred-gallon water tank in the basement and slowly got it filled from outside sources. A gas tank the same size was also added, as was a complete lathe, drill press, and workbench. The chemicals were stored in an airtight, compartmentalized box.

"Off the grid," was his only response to any of Wesley's questions. Finally, the old man fixed himself a place to live in the garage. There was still enough room for a half-dozen vehicles.

Wesley spent the next few weeks practicing—first, inside the place, so he knew every inch, especially how to get in and out unseen, even in daylight.

The last tile fell when Pet showed him the tunnel he had begun to construct.

"You can only use this *once*, Wes. It'll exit in the vacant lot on the corner of Water Street and the Slip. I'm going to fix it so's it's got about two feet of solid ground at its mouth, and then plank it up heavy. When you want to split that *one* time, you hit the depth-charge lever down here in your apartment, okay? That gives you a good ten minutes to get gone, and you'd better plan on using every second."

Wesley later expanded his investigations, making ever-widening circles away from the factory, but always returning within twelve hours. Pet got him a perfect set of identification. "You can always get a complete ID bun-

dle in Times Square. Good stuff, too. But the boys selling it usually roughed it off some poor bastard, maybe
totaled him, and it ain't worth the trouble. I know this
guy who makes the stuff from scratch, on government
blanks, too. A man like that, you pay what his work is
worth. You remember that."

Equipped with paper, Wesley could drive as well
as walk. He began to truly appreciate Carmine's "no
parole" advice.

When Pet came back one day, Wesley asked him
about another kind of practice. "I need to work with the
pieces. Where can I do it?"

"Right here. I got the fourth floor soundproofed. Anyway, with those silencers I made for you, you could blow
the wall away and not have anybody catch wise."

"What about practicing without the silencers?"

"What you want to do that for? All you'll get out of
removing the front end is more *noise*, that's all. Even
the long-range stuff has silencers now—I'll show you
later."

The old man was right. Wesley fired thousands of
rounds, making the most minute adjustments before
he was satisfied.

No one came around. No sirens, nothing.

It was easy to make the adjustments, since Pet had
the entire fourth floor marked off in increments of six
inches—ceiling, floors, and walls. Wesley worked out a
rough formula: the smaller the caliber, the more accurate the shot. The more bullets flying, the less accurate
each individual slug had to be. The closer to the target,
the less time you had to get ready.

Pet came back late one night, pressed the silent warning system to let Wesley know he was there, and was already making himself a cup of the vile black mixture he called "coffee" by the time Wesley got to the garage.

"I got something for you," the old man said. "It's a simple one. Probably just a test—I think they want to see if I can deliver."

"They think it's you going to be doing it?"

"Yeah, me and my 'organization,' right?"

"Right. Good. Tell me."

"It's a pawnshop right off Pleasant Avenue. The guy who runs it fronts for them. He's making good coin where he is, but he's a greedy fuck. When he started selling dope out of the place, he was stepping too close to the locals, and they dimed him out. He's looking at about a hundred years for what they nailed him with—he rolled over like a dog. But none of them know *we* know, so the feds are leaving him out there to get more—when it comes to info, they're as greedy as he was. They've even got an undercover working for him, right in the shop."

"Who's doing that?"

"A cop, from the CIB; a Puerto Rican kid, he looks like, but he's a cop for sure. Supposed to be a stock boy or something like that, but he uses that phone too much . . . and he ain't placing bets."

"So him, too?"

"Maybe more—the pawn guy's on the pad, and the beat bulls keep a close watch on his store. You know, so's he won't get taken off by some kid with a pistol."

"Can we get him over here some night?"

"Forget that! The first rule is that *nothing* gets done down here. We got to protect this territory completely. No dope fiends, no freaks, no fucking *nobody*, never. This is the safe house, understand? No, he's got to be hit right in his shop."

"Why not at his house, where he lives?"

"Too much pressure on the boys, it happens there. The Muslims have been giving this rat bastard hell because they know he's dealing. So we make it look like they did it."

"A white man in Harlem?"

"You thinking about him or you?"

"Me."

"Good. You ever use explosives?"

"Just grenades. In the Army."

"Same stuff. You light it, you throw it, and you get the fuck outta the way, right?"

"They might get out, too. No, wait a minute . . . are they both up front in the place?"

"Usually the cop stays in the back—but if he thinks you from the People, he'll drift up. So he'd be able to testify against you later."

"Doesn't this guy know who his contact is?"

"No. He's a small-time weasel. Any fucking hood comes in there with a 'message from the boys' and this faggot'll listen, you know?"

"Okay, when does the cop leave the place at night?"

"The guy we want opens up around ten. His cop helper gets there around noon. They work a long day, close up around eleven at night. We'll take the cab. Cost me twenty-eight large, but it's like being invisible."

Wednesday night, 9:10 p.m. A yellow medallion cab rolled up in front of the pawnshop, the old man at the wheel. Pet slid the cab down about four doors from the target and pulled out a newspaper. He poked a small hole in the middle of the paper with a sharp pencil, adjusted his rearview mirror until he was satisfied. Then he slipped the cab into gear and rested his left foot lightly on the brake; the rear brake lights did not go on.

Wesley climbed out of the back of the cab. He was dressed in a steel-gray sharkskin one-button suit with a dark-gray shirt and light-gray tie. His shoes flashed like black mirrors, in rhyme-time with the oversized white Lindy Star on his right pinky. His watchband matched his cufflinks, which matched his tie clip; his snap-brim fedora was pearl gray. He carried a small, round cardboard hatbox.

The bells above the door tinkled as Wesley entered. The shop was empty of customers. The pawnbroker was up front in the cage.

"Can I help you?"

"No, I can help *you*, pal. I got a message from the boys—they want you to take this package and . . ."

The Puerto Rican drifted toward the front as Wesley's voice trailed off.

"Who's this?" Wesley challenged.

"Oh, this is Juan, my stock boy. He's okay; he knows the score."

"Get him over here—I want to see his face."

Juan walked toward the front of the cage, smiling at the idea that this petty mobster wanted to see *his* face.

Wesley brought the 9mm Beretta out of the hatbox. The silencer made it seem six feet long, but Juan caught two slugs in the chest before he had a chance to wonder about it or make a move.

"Always take the hard man first—it's tougher on your guts, but if you take the soft man first, you won't be fucking alive to feel good behind it," Carmine had schooled Wesley, years ago.

Wesley immediately turned the gun on the other man, who flung his hands into the air. Wesley said, "Open the cashbox!" so the target would relax, and blew away the side of his face as the man bent toward the drawer.

Wesley put the hatbox down on the floor, clicked the snap-fuse open, and wheeled toward the door. He flipped the sign from "OPEN" to "CLOSED" and set the spring lock behind him as he went out. He was into the back seat of the cab and Pet was smoothly pulling away before Wesley could get the "Eight seconds!" out of his mouth.

They caught the first light and were headed east when they heard the explosion. Traffic stalled. Everyone tried to figure out where the noise had come from, but a cop, who empathized with any white man's desire to get the hell out of Harlem before dark, waved them through.

They hit the FDR rolling. The meter showed $4.65 by the time they neared the Slip.

"When we going to switch?" Wesley asked.

"We're not. Nobody's following us. I got a car buried on Park and Eighty-eighth and another in Union
Square, but we don't need them now. I'll pick them up
tomorrow. Change the numbers of this one tonight—
nothing to it. We don't want to make problems by getting too cute."

The late news had a story about a firebombing in
Harlem; the reporter said it looked like a "terrorist act."
The film clips showed the entire front of the pawnshop
and the stores on either side completely obliterated.
The firemen were still battling the blaze, and it was
not known if anyone had been inside at the time of the
explosion.

A full-regalia NYPD spokesman announced that a
confidential informant had told them that two men,
both Negro, of average height, were seen running from
the shop heading west just before the explosion. The
police expected arrests to follow.

"Were you the informant?" Wesley asked.

"You must be kidding, Wes. There's *always* some
righteous asshole who pulls that kind of number. Every
job I ever knew about had fifty fucking leads called in
that didn't have nothing to do with what actually went
down."

"Don't the cops know this?"

"And you Carmine's son! For Chrissakes, kid, don't
you know all they care about is making an arrest? They
could give a fuck about who's really guilty. Didn't you
get bum-beefed when you went down?"

"No. I did it, all right. I got ratted out by a scumbag
clerk in a hotel."

"Don't you want to pay him back?"

"Someday, when it ties in with something else. But I can't risk what we're doing just for payback."

"Good! Where is he?"

"Times Square."

"I can fucking guarantee you that sooner or later we'll get into his territory. I always hated to work down there, though. Those fucking freaks, you never know what they're going to do."

"I know what they're going to do."

"How the hell do *you* know?"

"One of them told me."

It was slightly more than a year later when Wesley asked, "How come they're paying a hundred K for this guy? What's so hard about him?"

"He used to run all the family business in Queens, but they had a sit-down and told him he's out. He took it the way he was supposed to, but there's still got to be a war over this—he still controls Queens, and they don't let you do that."

"Do what?"

"Keep tapping the till. He says he's not the boss, but his crew isn't going for that. This guy is *sharp*, now. No telephones, no mail. He lives in a fucking fortress out near the North Shore on the Island, and he runs the show from there."

"Can we get at him?"

"No way. I was by there myself a few times, and you'd have to fucking drop a *bomb* on the place. And even *that* might not work—he's got himself an air-raid shelter, left over from the Fifties.

"But he has to stay in touch. Got no choice. So, every month, he meets his capo on the Fifty-ninth Street Bridge."

"What? Right out in the open?"

"Yeah, Wesley, right out in the open. But it ain't just *him* that's out in the open. And we don't know what night he meets on. All we know is that it's always late. He gets a ride to the Queens side and meets the capo halfway across. On the walkway. He's got men on the Queens side, and his capo has cover on the Manhattan side."

"Couldn't we just drive past and hit him?"

"How? We don't know when he's coming, and if they see the same car pass back and forth, *we're* the ones who'll get hit. Besides, he stands with his back to the girders, and you couldn't get a decent shot at him, even if you could get on the bridge."

"How much time have we got?"

"If we get him before he wins the war, we get paid. If he loses the war first, we don't. If he wins the war, we *sure* don't."

"How long before the war starts? Out in the open, I mean."

"It may not start at all—they're still trying to nego-tiate. But they also want to cover all their bets, you know?"

"How come they don't try and cover *you*, with all the work you been doing for them?"

"They think they have. But they *also* think I got a

nice little organization of my own, with all old guys like me, and they don't want to *start* a war to prevent one. They're very slick, right?"

Wesley smiled. "Can you get me onto Welfare Island after dark?"

The old man nodded and got up to leave. Wesley climbed up to the fourth floor and took the rifle chambered for .219 Zipper from the gun rack. That cartridge had originally been designed for a lever-action Marlin— good enough for a varmint gun, but not for Wesley's work.

He had spent hours fitting the custom barrel to a full-bedded stock. Now it was a single-action weapon, and magnificently accurate. But he still couldn't make it hold a silencer, and he had more practicing to do.

Just as Wesley squeezed off another round, he noticed the orange light glowing immediately past his range of vision. Smoothly and calmly, he pulled the massive Colt Magnum from his shoulder holster and spun to face the door. It opened, and Pet stepped inside, a wide grin on his face. Wesley put the gun down and waited.

"Wes, I got a present for you," Pet said, displaying another rifle.

"What's that? I already got a good piece."

"You got nothing compared to this. This here's a Remington .220, the latest thing. It's got twice the muzzle velocity of that Zipper and it's more accurate, every time. And that's not the best part. I know a guy who works for the bullet people—he's a ballistics engineer. You know what he told me? He said that the engineers test-fire some slugs from every batch that the factory manufactures, to see if they're building the slugs up to the specs. Well, every once in a while they come across some that're just perfect, you know? They call these bullets 'freaks,' okay? And the engineers always take the whole batch and fire them themselves to see if they can figure out why these bullets work so good. Anyway, I got fifty rounds of those 'freaks,' just for this piece."

"I can make a three-inch group at seven hundred yards with the Zipper," Wesley said, doubtfully.

"The man told me he could double that distance and still group the same with this piece. And he's no marksman."

"Let me see it."

"Okay, kid. But remember, I only got fifty rounds."

"I'll test-fire it with some over-the-counter stuff first."

Four hours later, Wesley came down to the garage.

"Is it as accurate as the man said?" Pet asked him.

"Better. But it's the loudest damn thing I ever heard."

"So what? No point in silencing it anyway from the Island—the chumps on either shore'll think it was a backfire. We hit a guy like that once, years ago, me and Carmine. I set the car up so's it would backfire like a sonofabitch, right? So we're driving down the street with the car backfiring, and the creep ducks behind his bodyguards . . . but then they get wise it's only the car, and he starts laughing like a fool. He was still laughing when Carmine sent him a message, and the body-guards couldn't figure out what happened until we were around the corner."

"The engineer was sure right about this piece," Wesley said. "Any chance of getting some more slugs from him?"

"No. It was in the papers yesterday. Somebody must have wired his car. It blew up when he turned on the ignition."

Wesley and Pet replaced the stock of the new rifle. With a new cheek-piece, hand-sanded to micro-tolerances, it fit Wesley's face perfectly. He also had the latest night-scope: U.S. Army issue, and then only to jungle-sniper teams. Pet built a long black anodized-aluminum cone to hide the flash. Wesley mounted the piece on a tripod and sat comfortably behind it for a while. Then he disassembled the unit and climbed to the roof.

It was shadowy black on the waterfront as Wesley sighted in. He picked up a man and a woman in the scope, lying on the grass just off the river. The range was almost a mile, and Wesley carefully dialed in until he could see the man clearly. The nightscope worked to perfection: the man looked like he was in a spotlight against a dark background. The crosshairs focused on the man's upper chest, then on his face, and then on his left eye. Yes . . . there. With such a high-speed, low-density bullet, a chest shot wasn't a sure kill.

Wesley thought about the books he had read on triangulation and concluded that it would be possible for the cops to learn where the bullets had been fired from. Then he came to another, more significant conclusion: *So what?*

Pet was waiting in the garage.

"I got a kid," he told Wesley. "A good, stand-up kid. A *State* kid, you know? He'll bring a launch alongside the FDR. I'll be in the Caddy, pulled over like I got engine trouble. You can be into the launch in thirty seconds, and he'll bring you back about a mile upriver from there. And I'll be waiting."

"He'll see my face."

"You trust me?"

"Yes."

"He won't remember you."

"Him, too?"

"No. We'll need him again—he's one of us, I think. But I got something for him anyway, just in case."

"Can you find out which night the boss'll be on the bridge? Can you find out where I can shoot from?"

"I already got that much. But no time. That's all there's gonna be. Even *trying* to get more information would tip him."

"When do we start?"

"From tomorrow night until Thursday; that's as close as my guy knows. You ready?"

"Yes."

"You only get one shot. . . ."

"I haven't thought about that."

"Huh?"

"Tunnel vision's better for night work."

The battleship-gray Fleetwood purred northbound on the FDR. Then its engine began to miss and sputter. Pet pulled over to the side, went around to the front, and lifted the hood.

The kid came quietly out of the shadows.

"Here, Mr. P."

"I see you, kid. I *seen* you when I pulled in. Stay back further next time, right?"

"Yes, sir, Mr. P., I will."

"Okay, come here, kid, *quick!* I got something for you."

As the kid approached, Pet pulled a heavy metal-and-leather belt off the back seat of the Caddy. He motioned the kid forward and circled his waist with the belt. The front of the belt was a steel-tongued clamp, which Pet snapped closed.

"Try to get it open," Pet said.

The kid did try, hard, but he couldn't budge the clasp.

"It's full of plastic explosive, radio-controlled . . . with this," said Pet, holding up a small transmitter. "You understand?"

The kid's face didn't move a muscle—he just nodded.

"It won't go off no matter how hard it's hit, even with a bullet. But it *will* go off even if it's wet."

Pet slapped the kid lightly on the cheek, smiled, and winked at him like a father sending his son up to bat in a Little League game.

The trip to Welfare Island took less than three minutes. Wesley set up the long-armed bipod in the soft mud about a quarter-mile from the bridge. Pet told him it was possible to get even closer, but then he would be shooting almost straight up. Wesley already knew that depth perception is influenced by perspective and opted for the quarter-mile shot.

He used the hand-level with the glowing needle to get the bipod perfectly straight, then set up the rig, took a windage reading, and sighted in toward the middle of the bridge. It took another fifteen minutes of click-adjustments before he was completely satisfied.

The kid was good; he knew not to smoke, not to talk. They waited until 3:15 a.m. Nobody showed.

On the way back to the Slip, Wesley asked if the Island was really the best vantage point. "What about that Butler Lumber Millworks building on the Queens side?"

"I already checked it out, Wes. We'd have to leave about half a dozen people there if we tried it. We don't know *exactly* what night the man's gonna come, and that ain't the kind of stunt you can pull twice."

Wesley just nodded, not surprised.

By the third trip, Wesley could set the bipod and rig up in seconds instead of minutes. The kid was smoother, too. He had a pair of night glasses with him, and he was scanning the Queens side every thirty seconds, pausing just long enough to refocus each time.

At 1:05 a.m., he blew a sharp puff of air in Wesley's direction. Wesley immediately swung the scope toward the Queens end and saw the figure of a human walk-

ing toward the center of the bridge at moderate speed.
Maybe he's a jumper, he thought, but then another puff
of breath told him that someone was also approaching
from the other side. Wesley never took his eye off the
first man.

He watched with extreme care as the two men met
in the middle . . . and smoothly switched positions, so
that the man on the left was now the man from Queens.
A nice touch. Both men had their backs to the girders,
invisible from bridge traffic.

Wesley sighted in carefully, not knowing how much
time he'd have. A foghorn sounded somewhere up the
river, but the Island was quiet. The Harbor Patrol had
passed more than an hour ago, and they hadn't even
bothered to sweep Wesley's area with their spotlights—
although Wesley and the kid were well concealed against
the possibility.

The target's eyes were shielded by his hat. Wesley
sighted in on the lower cheek, figuring the bullet to
travel upward to the brain. He watched for the man's
lips to stop moving—he'd be less likely to move his head
if he was listening instead of talking. In between heartbeats, Wesley squeezed the trigger so slowly that the
earsplitting *cccrrack!* was a mild shock. The target was
falling forward before the sound reached the bridge.

The capo ducked down in anticipation of another
shot, but Wesley and the kid were halfway across the
river to the Manhattan side by the time the bodyguards
were fifty feet from the middle of the bridge.

When they landed, Pet quickly unhooked the kid's
belt, saying, "You were a man."

The kid just nodded. The outfit disappeared into the false bottom of the Caddy's back seat, and Pet had the big machine running toward Harlem in seconds. They caught the 96th Street turnaround, and were back in their own territory in another fifteen minutes.

"The kid had me covered good," Wesley told Pet, after they'd dropped him off. "He said there was another car that we could swim to if they hit the boat."

"Yeah," Pet replied. "He's the goods. And I don't think he did it just for the money, you know?"

It was two-ten in the morning as they turned into the factory block. Just before they got to Water Street, Wesley noticed a trio of men huddled in the mouth of an alley.

"Cops?" he asked.

"Junkies," Pet answered. "Dirty fucking junkies. They going to *bring* the motherfucking cops, though— they got no cover. We'll have to clear them the fuck outta here soon. How'd it go?"

"I hit him. That was all I could see—I didn't want to stay around. Would that belt you made the kid wear have worked?"

"Blow a six-foot hole in solid concrete."

"What's the range for the transmitter?"

"About a mile and a half . . . maybe two miles."

"Is that alley a dead end?"

"Yeah. And I can block it. But don't hit them here, for Chrissakes."

"Put the belt in the airline bag and give it to me.

Okay, now block the alley, and don't let any of them run."

Pet swung the Caddy smoothly across the alley's mouth, and Wesley was out of the car with the silenced Beretta pointed at all three men before they could move.

"Quick! Put your hands where I can see them."

"What is this, man? We're not—"

"Shut up. You want to make five hundred bucks?"

The smallest one stepped forward, almost into the gun. "Yeah, man. Yeah, we want to make the money. What we have to do?"

"Deliver this package for me. Just take it out on the Slip and walk through the jungle to the corner of Henry and Clinton. There'll be a man waiting for it there—he's *already* there. Then come back here and I'll pay you."

"You must think you're dealing with real fucking chumps, man! You'll pay us *after . . .*"

Wesley took five hundred-dollar bills from his pocket and held them out in his left hand, extending them toward the smallest one, who grabbed hold. Wesley didn't let go. "Take them and tear them in half. Neatly. Then give me back half."

"What the fuck for, man?"

"That way we're both covered, right? You come back, and by then my man has called and says he got the stuff. I get that call, you cop the other half of the bills. I'll pay you, all right—half of the fucking bills won't do *me* no good, and I don't want no beef with you guys anyway. Okay?"

"Okay, man, but . . ."

"But nothing. And either all three of you go or it's no deal."

"Why all three?"

"What if some fucking hijacker rips you off on the way over? You'll be safer that way, and *my* stuff'll be safer, too. But don't open the fucking bag—it's booby-trapped with a stick of dynamite."

"You *must* be kidding, man!"

"You think so, just open it up, sucker. But get the fuck away from me first."

With Wesley still holding the gun on him, the smallest one reached for the bills and carefully tore them, handing one half to Wesley. He looked up from his work and saw the glint of metal from the Caddy.

"Your partner got the drop on us, too, huh?"

Wesley didn't answer. The smallest one took the airline bag and pocketed the torn bills, then the three junkies walked out of the alley. The Caddy backed up just enough to let them by.

They turned toward the Slip. Wesley got in the Caddy and Pet pulled away. Using the night glasses, Wesley could pick out the three walking dead men as they moved toward Clinton Street.

Pet looked at his watch. "It takes a man about fifteen minutes to walk a city mile. Those dope fiends ain't no athletes—should take them about twenty to get to Henry Street."

Wesley said nothing; he was still watching the couriers to make sure they wouldn't split up and force him to go after whoever wasn't near the bag.

Pet wheeled the big car toward the garage. They were inside in seconds, and Pet climbed into the newly painted cab. "Still got about five minutes to go—I'm going out driving to make sure that stuff works."

"I'll be your passenger. I want to see if it works, too."

The cab was coming up Clinton toward Henry when Pet said, "Seven minutes—that's plenty," and pressed the transmitter's control button.

Explosion rocked the night. The cab raced toward Henry Street, but by the time they arrived, all they got to see were a few dismembered cars and a lamppost lying in the street. There was glass everywhere, reflecting all sorts of once-human colors.

Pet wheeled quickly and went the wrong way up Clinton to East Broadway, then raced uptown for a couple of minutes. He was back to normal late-night New York City cabbie speed by the time they crossed Grand Street.

"The miserable hypes must've wanted that money bad—they was *already* at Henry Street."

"I guess it worked."

"They'll need blotting paper to find them," Pet said. "Make sure you set fire to your half of the bills."

"I already did."

The morning news linked the bridge assassination to "mob sources," and the explosion on Henry Street to "long-simmering political differences between Latin gangs." Eleven people were reported killed and twenty-one others hospitalized.

Hobart Chan smiled to himself as his sable-and-tan Bentley rolled gently across the mesh grids of the Williamsburg Bridge and into the clogged traffic on Delancey Street. The air conditioning was whisper-quiet, the FM stereo filled the car's vast interior with soft string music, and its plushy tires transmitted not the slightest vibration to the driver's seat.

Chan preferred to drive himself into the city each day, although he could have quite easily afforded a chauffeur. It wasn't the expense that stopped him, or the paranoia that seemed to haunt the Occidental gangsters of his acquaintance. There were many trustworthy young Chinese boys coming over from Hong Kong every day. Good boys, not filled with the ancestor-worship crap that those born in Chinatown still seemed infected with. He used a number of them in his business. But there was just something so . . . perfect about the cloistered luxury of piloting his steel-and-leather cocoon past the degenerates and bums that filled the area along Forsyth, Chrystie, and Chan's personal favorite, the Bowery.

The experience was namelessly wonderful, and the corpulent little man loved it with a deep, private passion. He never missed an opportunity to make this soul-satisfying drive. As he crossed the bridge, the J train rumbled by in the opposite direction.

Hobart Chan was a firm believer in community control. Until he came from San Francisco seventeen years ago, *Cubanos* controlled prostitution in Chinatown through a tacit agreement with the Elders. But his willingness to launch a homicidal duel had finally resulted in a change of ownership.

Hobart Chan had run a lot of risks. But that was in the past. The risks were over, the *gusanos* were back dealing cocaine in Miami, where they belonged, and the flesh business had never been better.

Chan sometimes thought longingly about Times Square, but always concluded by writing off the idea. There was more money to be made there, true, and Chan was no stranger to the packaging and sale of human degeneracy . . . but something about that cesspool frightened him. Chan told himself that he was a businessman, and a good businessman didn't take *unnecessary* risks. So he remained content with the significant cash flowing into his Mott Street offices.

The only flicker of worry that ever crossed Chan's mind was about his new competition. Not all the young Chinese from Hong Kong wanted to work for the established organization, and he had been receiving threatening messages from some of the younger thugs. But Hobart Chan was too much a master of the art of extortion to fall victim to it himself. The new kids had no base outside of Chinatown, and they certainly weren't going to attack him *inside* his own territory.

As the big car crossed Grand Street, Chan decided he would drive down to the Bowery. The sight of dozens of pathetic humans in various states of decomposition, all running toward his car with filthy rags to "clean" his windshield in grateful exchange for whatever coins he wished to bestow, did more for him than even his occasional visits to his own merchandise.

He thought of his humble origins: the forged birth certificate that cost his father seven years of indentured servitude to enable the young Chan to enter the land of promise; the bloody-vicious mess in San Francisco; his eventual—in Chan's mind, inevitable—rise to power in his world.

As the Bentley approached Houston Street, Chan carefully slowed down. He never wanted to make the turn west on this light—it was the best corner for the display of bums. Once, he had thrown a dollar out his window after some of the lowlifes had attempted to clean his windshield, watching with fascination as they groveled in the street for the single piece of paper. Hobart Chan fancied that all the bums knew his car, and that they fought among themselves to see which of them would have the privilege of serving him each morning. Although it was difficult to imagine such human waste actually *fighting* for anything.

The bum that approached the car was younger than most, although no less degenerated. Chan mused on his theory that the entire race would someday find itself right down here on the Bowery, watching with concealed delight as the youngish bum industriously rubbed at the windshield and the side mirror with a foul rag. The bum was about thirty or thirty-five; it was hard to tell under the dark, stubbly beard and the rotted hat. This bum even carried a pint of what looked like clear vodka in his hand, holding on to it with a death grip.

Chan thought it somehow strange that a bum who

already *had* a bottle would still work to clean wind-shields like this. Somehow it seemed even more debas-ing than usual.

The bum quickly finished and looked beseechingly at Hobart Chan. The fat man's jade-ringed finger touched the power-window switch, and the glass zipped down on its greased rails. As Chan extended the crisp dollar bill, the mouth of the bum's vodka bottle seemed to fly open—the contents gushed out all over the flesh mer-chant's custom-made suit.

Chan's face twisted into an ugly mass. He was draw-ing back his left hand to slap the bum when he noticed that the vodka smelled like gasoline.

That was the last conscious thought printed on his brain as the bum tossed a flaming Zippo lighter into the front seat and was off running with the same motion.

There was a brief sound like heavily compressed air being released; then the flames enveloped the interior of the big car. Chan screamed like a mad beast and ripped at the door handle—the door was stuck. He frantically pushed against the door, but the flames held him pris-oner for another second or so. Until they reached the gas tank.

The only witnesses to Wesley's departure were the bums.

The cab pulled up at the far end of the alley, and Wesley caught it at a dead run. He dived into the back seat and began wiping his hands with the damp towels there. Pet turned toward Houston and took the main drag to Sixth Avenue. He followed Sixth Avenue north and wound his way through the Village until he got to Hudson Street.

He followed Hudson to Horatio, where he parked the cab and both men got out. They climbed into a black Ford. The kid slipped from behind the Ford's wheel and into the front of the cab. He was wearing a chauffeur's cap today, but no belt. The Ford swung uptown, Wesley in the front seat, Pet driving.

"That epoxy stuff is perfect, Pet. It sealed the door like cement."

"I told you it would. Even with a few coats of wax on the doors, it'll always work."

"I could have sat there and pumped slugs into him for days. Nobody sees nothing down there."

"They paid for him to die by fire, not bullets, right?"

"Yeah," Wesley mused. "I wonder how those kids put together all that money."

Wesley was lying on his back on his kitchen floor, his hands working under the sink, when he heard the soft buzz from the console near the front door. The Doberman soundlessly trotted into position, left of the narrow door. Wesley flipped on the TV monitor and saw Pet coming down the long corridor. Only Pet knew how to set off the buzzer, but he wanted to make sure the old man was alone.

Satisfied, he hissed at the dog to get its attention, saying "okay" in a hard, flat, deliberate voice. The dog would tolerate Pet alone, but would attack him as quickly as anyone else if he approached Wesley without seeing a warn-off.

Wesley pushed the toggle switch forward, and the door slid away, leaving an opening large enough for a man to get through sideways. Pet came in, and the door closed tightly behind him. The old man looked at the assorted tools spread over the kitchen floor.

"What you up to?"

"I'm fixing the dog's food. He gets it by pushing this lever; gets water by pushing the other one. I got about a fifty-day supply, and I'm going to fix it so's he gets a dose of sleep-forever on the last one."

"What the hell for?"

"If I don't come back one time, he'll run out of food sooner or later and he'll starve to death. He don't deserve to go out like that."

"I could come in here and feed him for you."

"That's what you *will* do before the last day, if you're around then."

"Maybe you can read minds."

"What's that mean?"

"There's a job order out with my name on it."

"The same people?"

"Yeah. That's their way. I've done too much work for them, and now I get thrown in against another organization, like they think I got. The winner gets to keep working for them; the loser don't. They don't trust nobody. The last thing they want is for the top independents to get together, you know?"

"That's what Carmine said it would be like. He said if I got real good that's what they'd do."

"Yeah, only Carmine *knows* these weasels. He's way ahead of them. Even if they get me, you're still on the street and they'll never see you coming."

"Why you making out a will, old man?"

"You ever hear of The Prince?"

"Yeah. I have. So?"

"That's their man for this one. He'd never come in here after me, even if he knew where I was. But if I want to work, I have to go where they send me. So they'll give me a job in the cesspool, and he's like a fish in the water there."

"You're not supposed to know about the order out for you?"

"No."

"Who told you?"

"Nobody. But I put it together easy enough. All of a sudden, they got a job for me in Times Square. Only one thing that can mean—they got The Prince on the case. They never told me *where* to hit a mark before, but they got some bullshit story about only being able to get this guy when he comes outta one of them massage parlors. They must think I'm a Hoosier."

"And you're not?"

"What the fuck does that mean?"

"Carmine always said if you're *ready* to die you're dangerous, but if you're *looking* to die you're nothing to worry about."

"I ain't looking to die, but that fucking pit is impossible to work in. And if I turn down this job, they'll just hit me when I show my face on the street anytime after that. I can't stay in here forever."

"You ever think about just retiring or something?"

"And do what? Go fishing in fucking Miami? I'll retire the same way Carmine did—the same way you're going to—but I'd like to fucking retire this Prince cocksucker before I do. Then they'll never forget my name."

"What's he look like?"

"I only saw him once. He's a fucking giant stick. About six-four, maybe a hundred-twenty pounds, with hair like that Prince Valiant in the comics. That's where he got the name. Diamonds all over him—wristwatch, ID bracelet, cufflinks, belt buckle, everything. He's got monster hands, about twice as big as mine. Skin's dead white, like yours was when you got out. Like he's never *been* out. In the daytime, he probably hasn't."

"Can you get close?"

"No way. He's got that cesspool wired. Nothing goes down from Port Authority to Forty-ninth, Broadway to the Hudson, that he don't know about. Every fucking freak on the street reports to him."

"He should be easy to spot, right?"

"Sure. But he'd have me spotted first."

"He don't know me."

"No, but so what? You want to hit him alone?"

"He's just a man."

"If that's all he was, I wouldn't be worried about this. He's a fucking *freak*, I told you. Only a freak could live down there like he does."

"Where down there?"

"I don't know. He keeps different boys all the time, but he always sticks them in some fleabag flophouse. There's a hundred ways outta those rat-traps . . . if you know about them."

"I know about them. I was staying in one when I got popped for the last bit."

"Okay. But he knows *all* of them, Wes, every fucking one."

"Stay inside tonight. I'm gonna go in there and look. Get me some upstate plates for the Caddy."

Wesley returned to working under the sink, and Pet left him alone to go prepare the car. Just past midnight, Wesley wheeled the Caddy up Water Street and turned left onto Pike. He traveled crosstown until he crossed Broadway, connected with the West Side Highway, and rolled uptown. He exited at 23rd Street and followed Twelfth Avenue north to 42nd. There, he left the Caddy with the attendant at the Sheraton; he already had a late-arriving reservation . . . and a light suitcase.

In his room, Wesley changed into wine-red knit slacks and a flaming Hawaiian-print shirt worn loose outside the pants. He added a pair of genuine alligator loafers and an ID bracelet on a thick sterling chain. The initials were "CT." He left his pistol in the Caddy and the flick knife in his suitcase.

At one-fifteen, he started his walk. He strolled past Dyer, trying to get a fix on the territory. Neon smashed at him with every step.

LIVE BURLESQUE
CHANNEL 69
MERMAID

42ND STREET CINEMA
TOM KAT THEATRE

The street was alive the way a can of worms is alive: greasy and twisty-turning, but not going anywhere, comfortable only in the dark. As he crossed Tenth Avenue, Wesley noticed that the West Side Airlines Terminal was closed. A closer look told him that it was closed for good. Wesley looked up at the fifth floor; it would give a commanding view of the ugly scene below. For a flash-second, he thought about Korea.

Wesley crossed Ninth Avenue and headed down toward Eighth. He noticed five phone booths on the south side of the street and the Roxy Hotel on the north side. It was the Roxy where he got busted years ago, and he had to fight down the urge to see if the same clerk was still on duty . . . hands always ready to call the cops. Some other time.

As he crossed Eighth, Wesley reflected that the Parole Board was just a couple of blocks away, right near the Port Authority. They never closed. He could have just walked in there and asked a question like any other citizen, but that thought never occurred to him.

He could tell a cop at a glance, and he assumed that reaction was reversible. He noted the big Childs Restaurant on Eighth and 42nd, but didn't stop in. He counted thirteen movie houses between Eighth and Seventh. Thousands of people were on the street. Wesley wasn't even picking up second glances from the traffic flow.

"When I'm on the street, how do I make sure the

hustlers don't make me?" Wesley had asked Lester years ago. The answer was simple: "Just *stare* a lot. Squares can't *stop* staring at us, even when they know they shouldn't."

Crossing Broadway, Wesley almost walked right into The Prince, who was coming out of Rexall's. The Prince wasn't alone. His huge right hand was resting possessively on the back of his companion's neck—a short, powerfully built black guy with a monster Afro and a diamond earring in his right ear.

Wesley followed them down Broadway. The Prince was continually being stopped, and his progress was slow. Wesley watched closely, but all The Prince did was occasionally lay money on people who apparently asked for some—nothing else.

But then he suddenly stopped a fat woman, and Wesley halted about a half-block behind them. They held a quick, whispered conversation, making no attempt to hide the fact that their communication wasn't meant for bystanders, The Prince still holding the back of the black guy's neck. The woman nodded vigorously as though she understood, and then continued up the block in Wesley's direction.

As she approached, she focused her eyes directly on Wesley and picked up speed. He could have avoided her rush but made no attempt to—it would have been out of character to even have noticed.

The fat woman body-slammed Wesley, knocking him back against a mailbox. She gasped, grabbing huge handfuls of Wesley's Hawaiian shirt to steady herself. As she attempted to rise, she pulled the shirt up almost to his neck and then slapped her hands against his chest for a second before she quickly ran them along his body, across his groin, and down almost to his knees. Wesley struggled to get free, felt his pants lift over his socks, saving her that trouble. He cursed vehemently, and the fat woman backed off with some mumbled drunken apologies.

It had been a lovely, professional frisk. She'd be able to tell The Prince he wasn't heeled, wired, or dangerous.

Wesley brushed himself off and hurried up the block. He passed by The Prince and threw him a frankly curious glance, like any tourist would. The Prince continued down the block. Using a store window for a mirror, Wesley saw the giant step into a phone booth. He didn't see The Prince deposit any money, so he assumed it was the fat woman calling in to report.

Wesley turned up 46th Street and got a cab downtown on Fifth. He told the driver to take him to the Village, not knowing how far The Prince's network went. He entered the hotel on Bleecker between Sullivan and West Broadway and walked to a room he had registered the day before.

He telephoned Pet. The cab took him back to the Sheraton and dropped him off. He checked out the next morning, paying his bill in cash.

Pet was waiting in the garage. Neither of them liked to return in the daytime and avoided it whenever possible.

"You see him?" the old man asked.

"Yeah. How does he make a living? If he's dealing, he must have every cop in the precinct greased—you can't miss him."

"He does the same work you do."

"You know anything about a black guy, his boy-friend?"

"No. But I know he always marks his boyfriends with one of his diamonds. They get to wear the diamond so long as they're in with him. When they show on the street without the diamond, it means he's done with them. After that, they're nothing but a fucking piece of meat. He's got a new one every couple months or so."

"Could the kid live down there a couple a weeks and watch the black guy?"

"I don't think so, Wes. That's a real freak show, and the kid might panic if one of them made a move on him."

"You're right. One of them moved on me last night."

"What happened?"

"This was on my way back to the Sheraton. I was waiting for the light to change, and this freak comes up and asks me if the CT on the ID bracelet stands for 'cock-teaser,' right?"

"Jesus! I told you you shouldn'ta worn that. . . ."

"Hey, look, Pet, he just wanted to hit on me, period. No matter what fucking initials I'd've had, he would've said *something*."

"You have to hurt him?"

"On the street? I told him I'd meet him in the last row of the Tom Kat at midnight."

"The Tom Kat?"

"Some sleazo movie joint I saw on the way down."

The old man laughed. "I can't see the kid doing that. Where he was raised, he'd've opened up that freak for sure."

"You got to forget your image if you want to move out there. That's something you have to be taught, and Carmine taught me. Now . . . what happens if you lay up for a couple a weeks without doing anything? Will they think you lost your nerve?"

"Nah, they'll think I'm getting ready to go on in."

"Would The Prince want to make it personal?"

"What do you mean?"

"Would he have to hit you himself? Or could any of his freaks do it?"

"He'd want to hit me himself. It'd mean a lot if he did. You take a man out, you take his rep for yours."

"What's he use?"

"Mostly his hands. He's one of those karate experts. He never carries himself, but some of his freaks are always around, and they all shoot or stab. But The Prince, he works small. They say he can kill you with anything: a rolled-up newspaper, a dog chain, you know what I mean."

"So he'd have to be close. And we don't."

"You could never pop him from one of the buildings. He'd know you was inside before you even got set up. Did he see your face last night?"

"So what? He didn't know who I was."

"He will if he ever sees it again," Pet said solemnly. "You can forget about getting close, Wes."

"All right. Stay here for a few days—I'm going out to look at him good this time."

Wesley spent the next six nights driving the cab in Times Square, catching only occasional glimpses of The Prince, and always at a distance. But he did locate the black man with the diamond earring, and the black man had a pattern. Too much of a pattern—whatever else he was, Wesley knew he wasn't a professional.

Every night, just before eleven, he went to Sadie's Sexational Spa ("THE BEST IN THE WESTside"), on Eighth between 44th and 45th. He stayed about a half-hour each time.

He went in different directions after that—never the same way. Wesley followed him three times, and each time he met The Prince, always on the street or at the entrance to one of the bars.

Wesley returned to the garage a little after midnight on Wednesday. Pet came out of the shadows and walked over to the cab.

"Can we do it?" the old man wanted to know.

"Yeah, but it's gonna be sticky. You're going to have to go in there with a car. Go in *fast*, and get out before he can move. We need him to know you're on the case, like you're going to drive-by him and the cruise is about setting it up."

"Why you want him like that?"

"Misdirection. Like with the backfiring car you told me about."

"Okay. Then what?"

"The rest is mine. You just wait with the car. No, bump that—how many cars can you plant in different spots around the cesspool?"

"If I started now, I could probably get about six, 'specially if the kid helps."

"Okay, we'll use under the West Side Highway Bridge by the river. On Fortieth, and Thirty-third, and Twenty-third. And Forty-second and Fifth, and anyplace else you think is good. Get the list where you got them stashed, and get ready to go out in the cab by eight-thirty tomorrow night. I'm going to sleep."

"Wesley . . ."

"What?"

"We give the kid a key, then he could take care of the dog if—"

"The dog would kill him."

The yellow cab rolled up Eighth Avenue, Pet driving, Wesley the back-seat passenger, dressed in a khaki fatigue jacket and heavy twill cargo pants, tucked into soft-soled field boots. Under the jacket, he wore a black Ban-Lon pullover with long raglan sleeves.

In the side pocket of the pants he carried two identical knives; the blades extended back through the handles and were anchored by a tiny metal bead. Zipped into the inside pocket of the field jacket was a .25 Beretta. One outside pocket held a screw-on silencer. Another held two full clips of custom rounds: hardballs with sealed iodine tips.

Swinging from the thin webbing belt was a pair of baseball-sized fragmentation grenades. The front pocket of the pants held a Colt Cobra .38 with a two-inch barrel.

Wesley was additionally equipped with a small plastic bottle of talcum powder, four pairs of rubber surgeon's gloves, and a black silk handkerchief. Clipped to the back of the webbing belt was a pair of regulation police handcuffs. Also on board was a thousand dollars in bills, from singles to centuries, a soft pack of Marlboros, a disposable butane lighter, and a miniature propane torch.

Sewn into Wesley's left sleeve were registrations for the six cars, as well as a valid FS-1 for each. He carried only a single key, which would start any of the vehicles. He also carried a driver's license, a Social Security card, an Army DD 214 form, a membership card in Local 1199 of the Hospital Workers Union, and a clinic card showing that his next appointment was for Monday at the VA Hospital on 24th and First.

He had spent twenty-four hours a day for three weeks dressed exactly the same way, and knew he could move without giving the slightest hint of all the extra weight.

The cab stopped on 44th, and Wesley got out. It was ten-fifteen.

Wesley entered Sadie's. A red light glowed against the far wall. Beneath it, a fat man with a menacing face sat behind a scarred wooden desk. The fat man's face lit up with what was supposed to be both a smile of welcome and a warning.

"Can I help you, buddy?"

"I want a massage."

"Twenty-five bucks in front. You pay *me* for the massage—that buys you twenty minutes. Anything extra—more time, whatever—you settle with the girl, okay?"

"Okay."

"Now, take a look in this here book and tell me whicha the girls you want."

He showed Wesley the kind of album proud mothers keep of weddings. There were about forty pages, with two devoted to each girl. Wesley watched as the man thumbed through it. They all looked alike. Wesley's finger stabbed at random.

"How about that one?"

"Sorry, buddy, this is Margo's night off. But if you like blondes, how about *this*?" He displayed a well-worn eight-by-ten glossy with obvious pride. The merchandise was lying down on a couch, nude, and looking straight into the camera's eye. She looked about sixteen.

"Yeah, okay. Is she ready now?"

"Sure, just hold on a minute. *Joanne!*" he bellowed. A girl who vaguely resembled the picture in the album came into the front area to escort Wesley back to a booth. He couldn't see her face, but he saw she moved like she was thirty-five and tired. She ushered Wesley into what looked like a large closet: plasterboard walls, an Army cot with folded sheets, a pillow without a case, a tiny lamp with a pink low-watt bulb, a cracked porcelain bowl half full of tepid water. The girl pulled her shift over her head. She was wearing what looked like the bottom half of a bikini and several pounds of flesh-colored powder.

"Why don't you just lie down on the bed there and tell me what you'd like, honey?"

Wesley's watch said 10:28.

"Come here."

"Sure, honey, but you know that'll cost you extra, right?"

"Right." Wesley motioned for the girl to sit beside him on the cot; he took out two hundred-dollar bills and folded them flat across her knee.

The girl nervously licked her lips and gave him a half-smile. "Honey, I know this is Times Square and all . . . and I can show you a real nice time . . . but for that kind of money maybe you want one of the other girls here, I don't—"

"You can earn this, and another two hundred on top, just for being quiet and helping me a little bit."

"What do you mean? Listen, I don't go—"

"Just take the money and keep quiet. I need some answers and some help. I can pay you for that . . . or I can cut your fucking throat."

The razor-edged knife was nestled against the girl's carotid artery before Wesley finished the sentence. He watched her eyes to make sure she wasn't going to panic or scream.

"No noise, okay?" he said quietly. "Just no noise and some answers. Then I'm gone and you scored the four hundred."

The woman said nothing.

"Every night, just before eleven, a short, husky black guy comes in here. He's got a big Afro and a diamond earring in his right ear and—"

"I know who he is, that sicko."

"Yeah. Okay, who's he go with?"

"*Anyone*, man. For what he does, he can't be choosy. You know what he wants to—"

"I don't care what he wants. I want *him*. I want to *talk* to him, you understand? Alone. Just for five minutes."

"What do you want *me* to do?"

"You got two choices. I could cut you real quiet and just wait for him back here . . . or you could go out front and bring him back here with you."

"I'll bring him back. He'd like to go with me. He asked me before. I could—"

"Just relax. Look at this: you know what it is?"

He held the Beretta in one hand, the knife still at her throat with the other.

"I know what it is."

"Do the other girls get angry if you take a customer?"

"Nobody would get mad if I took *him*. They only take him in here at all because he's got a real strong friend in the Square."

"I know all about his friend—that's who I work for. I'm here to take the diamond outta that nigger's ear, you understand?"

"Why didn't you just say so, man? I know the score. You don't need the knife, I'll—"

"You wait in the doorway," Wesley cut her off, pointing. "Right there. When he comes in, you bring him back here with you. You say anything to the fat man, you scream, you throw a signal—*anything*—and I'll put a bullet in your spine before you finish."

"Okay, okay, stop *talking* like that. Give me another twenty-five."

"For what?"

"So's I can go out and tell Harry that you're paying for another session—that way he won't bother you. Then I'll tell him you're getting cleaned up, so he won't wonder about you being back here, okay?"

"Okay. Go ahead."

Wesley's alternative plan was to shoot both the girl and the manager and be waiting at the desk when the black man came in. If she did anything bogus, he'd have the decision made for him. He screwed in the silencer, making sure the girl saw it, gave her another twenty-five dollars, and watched from the doorway as she walked to the desk.

"Here's another payment, Harry. Client wants another session."

"Good. Make this one shorter, understand?"

"Sure, Harry, but I want to work him for a tip, too."

"Bitch, you work for *me*, not the fucking customers, understand?"

"Okay, Harry, sure. I'll get him out soon."

The manager went back to his newspaper. Wesley thought he must have incredible eyesight to read in that dim light. Joanne returned to the room, walking past Wesley, who was still in the doorway.

"I did it."

"I heard. Is he going to get weird if the black guy comes back here with you without me leaving yet?"

"Man, I thought you knew what that guy's scene was. Harry wouldn't *expect* you to come out."

"Okay. Now just be quiet, and wait."

They sat in silence as the front door opened. It wasn't the black guy. The new customer seemed to know who he wanted and sat down to wait. In a couple of minutes, a tall, rail-thin girl came out of one of the other rooms, and he followed her back. It was 10:48.

The door opened again. It was the black man, wearing a red velour jumpsuit and red shoes with four-inch platform heels. Joanne slipped past Wesley and switched her hips into the front room. The black man looked up as she entered. Joanne smiled and motioned with her hand.

"Changed your mind?" the black man asked.

"A girl can, can't she?"

The black man followed her back toward the room. Wesley was just walking out of the same doorway. As they moved past him, Wesley wheeled and whipped the Beretta's butt viciously into the black man's kidney. The black man pitched forward into the tiny room, the girl just ahead of him. They went down in a sprawl of bodies. Neither made any effort to get up. The girl knew enough to stay quiet, and the black man was transfixed by the extended barrel of Wesley's pistol.

"No noise," Wesley told him.

"What is this?"

"It's a quiz show. You give me the right answers and you win a big prize."

"Don't be stupid, man. You know who I am?"

"Yeah. I do. But you're not the one I want—he is."

Wesley pulled the handcuffs from the webbing belt

and walked toward the black man, who extended his wrists as though he'd been through the routine a thousand times. Wesley slammed one cuff over the black man's right wrist, and snapped the other over the girl's left before she could react.

"Hey!" she yelped.

"Shut up. It won't be for long. I don't want either of you to move. Now, we've got about ten minutes for you to tell me what I need to know," he said to the black man.

"And what's that?" the black man said, still calm and in control.

"You're going to meet The Prince when you leave here. Where?"

"Man, you're not serious!"

Wesley leveled the piece at the girl's forehead and squeezed the trigger. There was a soft, ugly *splat!* and her body slumped, almost pulling the black man with her. The black man frantically shifted his weight to keep away from the blood. He couldn't see any, but he knew it would start flowing any second.

"I'm *very* serious," Wesley said softly. "The next one's yours."

"Man, don't do anything like that, listen. . . ."

Wesley deliberately cocked the pistol, held it in both hands, and pointed at the black man's upturned face. He tightened his facial muscles as he carefully took aim.

"Under the Times clock! On Forty-third. Between Seventh and Eighth! *Don't!*"

"What time?"

"Eleven-thirty."

"Who gets there first?"

"He does, man. He always—"

The bullet interrupted the black man. His death was as soundless as the shot. Wesley shifted the piece to his left hand and squatted by the bodies. He carefully slit each throat and wiped the blade on the velour jumpsuit. He shook talcum powder onto his hands and pulled on a pair of the surgeon's gloves. Then, still holding the gun, he wiped every surface in the room he had touched with the black handkerchief, and gathered up the spent cartridge cases—it took only about forty-five seconds. He knelt by the door to listen; there was still no sound from the front room.

Wesley slipped down the corridor. As he entered the front room, he saw that the clock over the desk read 11:20—his own watch said that was a couple of minutes fast. The fat man at the desk looked up as Wesley approached.

"Just about to *call* you, buddy."

Wesley fired. The first slug caught the fat man in the chest; his head dropped to the desk. The second bullet entered the top of his head. Wesley was about to walk out the door when he remembered the Marine and put another bullet into the fat man's left ear socket.

Even in the thin-walled parlor, the shots were virtually soundless. Wesley exchanged clips, then carefully pocketed the spent casings.

Wesley turned right on 43rd. He noticed the clock in the package store said 11:23—his own watch tallied, and he slowed his stride slightly. The still-assembled piece was now tucked into his belt, over his stomach. By sharply drawing a breath, he could pull it free without trouble.

He lay back in the shadows until he saw 11:29 on his watch, then mentally counted to fifteen and started to walk up the right-hand side of the block toward the Times Building. The big digital clock read 11:31, and he saw The Prince standing underneath, legs spread and arms extended. His left hand gripped his right wrist—Wesley could see the diamond-flash.

One hundred feet. The Prince was focused on him now, but the Wesley he had seen before was a tourist geek in a Hawaiian shirt. Wesley padded softly forward on the dark street: the silenced pistol wasn't accurate past twenty feet.

Fifty feet. Suddenly, The Prince spun and took off up the street. Wesley sprinted after him. The silenced pistol cut into his groin, but he didn't slow—if The Prince got to contact one of his freaks, the whole thing would be over.

The Prince wasn't used to running—by the corner of 43rd and Eighth, Wesley was only about ten yards behind. His target glanced west for a split second, then, seeming to understand that he was running out of cesspool in that direction, he turned north on Eighth and dashed across 44th toward the Playbill Bar. Wesley hit the bar just seconds behind The Prince, spotted him trying for the phone booth to the left of the door, and brought the gun up. The Prince caught the movement and dived for the Eighth Avenue door.

Wesley backed out the way he'd come in, and hit Eighth just in time to see The Prince flying up the west side of the wide avenue. It was clogged with people. The Prince slid smoothly through the human traffic, but he couldn't disappear. And he knew Wesley was too close for him to stop and get help.

The Prince dashed into the custard stand on 49th and Eighth and immediately exited out the side door. He tore up the side street toward the river. Wesley was close enough now but running too fast to get a clear shot. The Prince looked back quickly without breaking stride and jumped the fence that enclosed the parking lot between 49th and 50th. He was halfway across the lot, heading toward Polyclinic Hospital, when Wesley stopped, braced himself, and fired—but The Prince was bobbing and weaving, and the shot missed.

Wesley clawed his way over the fence and set himself for another shot, but The Prince picked up the shadow-change and veered sharply left just before the hospital entrance, steaming up 50th toward Ninth, with Wesley close behind.

The Prince turned right again at Ninth, just slightly ahead of Wesley, who could now run faster with his gun out. Between 50th and 51st was a construction site, partially excavated. The expensively painted sign read something about YOUR TAX DOLLARS.

The Prince was over the fence and into the site in a heartbeat. He looked back and couldn't see Wesley. For the first time since he'd been spooked, The Prince felt a quick jolt of fear penetrate the adrenaline.

Wesley had seen The Prince's move. He rushed up

50th instead of going up Ninth, so he was into the site before The Prince.

The streetlights didn't penetrate the excavation—the same kind of soft, dull darkness Wesley remembered from Korea. He lay prone in the weeds, motionless and listening. It was a simple equation: The Prince had to be close to kill, and Wesley didn't have the luxury of shooting from a distance.

Wesley could hear the street noises above him, but they were normal. He was alone. So was The Prince.

Wesley heard the sound grass makes when it's pushed against the way it normally grows. He forced himself *not* to relax. He could lie there for hours without moving, and The Prince couldn't come up on him without getting blown away. But he didn't *have* a long time.

If The Prince got out of the site, he'd have a hundred freaks surrounding the place in a few minutes. But if he stood up and ran for the fence, he was as good as dead. And he wasn't used to waiting.

Wesley focused, blocking out everything but the sounds of movement. As soon as he picked them up, he fired twice in that direction. The silenced bullets were only slightly amplified by the depression in the ground—Wesley heard them whine close to the earth. The movement had been about thirty yards away from him when he fired.

The next movement was closer—The Prince had made his choice. Wesley fired three times, as fast as he could pull the trigger. The site was a bowl of quiet inside the street noises. Wesley started to thrash around as if in a panic, making it clear where he was.

He heard another movement—about twenty feet away this time. The Prince, probably moving the grass with a stick. Wesley scanned for any diamond-flash, but all he picked up was the same darkness—he guessed the target had made the sacrifice.

Wesley pulled the trigger rapidly. The whine faded to a dry, audible *click!* as the firing pin hit air. "Fuck!" Wesley snarled, in a voice just past a whisper but bloated with panic. He viciously threw the gun at a spot about ten feet away and sprang to his feet, the now unarmed assassin lost without his weapon.

Wesley made all the sounds of a terrified man trying to remember to make as little noise as possible. He rolled onto his back and started pushing himself toward 51st Street with his legs, the two-inch Colt now in his right hand.

The Prince flew out of the darkness in a twisting, spinning series of kick-thrusts, offering only a narrow target in case his would-be assassin still had a knife. He was about eight feet away when he saw the pistol; he threw himself flat on his back, already tucking his shoulder under to kick upward when the X-nosed slug caught him in the chest, pinning him to the ground.

The noise from the two-incher was deafening. And, magnified by the bowl, it was cannon-like. All the street noises seemed to stop in unison. Wesley walked slowly toward The Prince, and saw he was choking on his own blood—the slug must have caught a lung.

"A . . . million dollars," The Prince gasped. "A million if you don't finish me, man. Just . . ."

The Prince launched himself off the ground, the

knife-edge of his hand extended. Wesley saw it all in slow motion—he had plenty of time to squeeze out another round, slamming The Prince back to earth. Wesley walked toward him calmly, emptying the pistol. Two shots to the face, the third into the throat.

The street noises were getting much louder. Wesley quickly reloaded, pocketing the empties. He scanned the field, looking for the silenced Beretta, but gave it up in a second—it wasn't carrying his prints, and the darkness that hid it from The Prince hid it just as effectively now.

Wesley pulled the pin on one of the grenades and held it tightly in his right hand. With his left, he pulled The Prince's hands up until they were on either side of what had been his face.

Wesley stuffed the grenade into where The Prince's mouth should have been and released the lever.

By the time the blast echoed throughout the city canyon, Wesley was at the perimeter of the site. As he slid under the fence, he saw a crowd of people outside Lynch's Bar on the corner . . . and heard a squad car's siren. He looked to his left, toward the river, and saw that way was still clear. Wesley threw himself prone and unsnapped his last grenade. He pulled the pin and held the lever closed in his right hand. With his left, he aimed the pistol carefully at the big cop trying to hold back the crowd.

The revolver boomed twice. Wesley was up and lobbing the grenade before the crowd started to panic and run. It arced through the night under the streetlights, then exploded. Wesley was already running toward

Tenth Avenue off the follow-through from his throwing motion. He knew that the closest car was at 40th and Twelfth. And that he only had a minute or two to disappear into the shadows. He kicked his legs high into his chest, trying desperately for a burst of speed that wouldn't come.

As he crossed Eleventh Avenue, a cab flashed its lights off and on twice. Wesley turned toward it, the little revolver up and ready. He ran toward the driver's window and was only half surprised to see Pet behind the wheel. He was into the cab and Pet was heading downtown before Wesley could catch his breath. The cab turned left on 23rd and headed crosstown.

"What were you doing there?" he finally asked Pet.

"I was cruising Twelfth all night. When the scanner said there was a report of shots fired in the construction site, I figured it was you. I knew Fortieth and Twelfth was the closest car, and you wouldn't be trying to go crosstown to Fifth with all that heat around."

"What if I didn't come out?"

"I was going in."

"After me?"

"After that Prince motherfucker."

The cab hit the FDR Drive and grabbed the service road. They were back onto the Slip and into the garage by 12:15. The police-band was still screaming *"Code Three!"*

The *Post* had a bylined story on the riot in Times Square the night before. Police theorized that it was a terrorist attack of some kind, probably aimed directly at the

"Guardians in Blue." There was no mention of a man found in the construction site. Pet looked up from the paper at Wesley, who was staring with fixed concentration at a completely blank white wall.

"There's nothing in here about The Prince," the old man said.

"Why should there be?" Wesley asked. "There couldn't be that much left of him."

"They always got fingerprints . . . dental charts . . . *something*."

"With any kind of luck, they won't get either off him. But maybe some of his freaks took him away and buried him."

"What do I tell them?"

"The People?"

"Yeah."

"Tell them he's gone. They hear your voice, they'll already know you're not."

"How did I do it?"

"None of their fucking business, right? You don't get paid to draw blueprints—that's not professional, anyway."

"I'll go upstairs and call them—might as well get things rolling," Pet said. "There's going to be a council behind this for sure. They won't admit what they tried to set up, but with The Prince dead, they'll know I know . . . something."

"You know where the meet is going to be?"

"You never know in front. They'll just find me on some corner with a car and take me there . . . then drop me off when it's over."

"Could I follow them with the cab?"

"No way. *I* might be able to do it . . . *maybe* . . . but not you. It takes years to be that good with cars."

"Could we find out where from someone?"

"You think this is the fucking movies? Forget it. In forty years doing their work, the only thing like that I ever found out was where Salmone's daughter lives. And even that was a fucking accident."

"The big guy? His daughter?"

"Yeah. His natural daughter, only she's changed her name and everything. She lives on Sutton Place, in one of those co-ops, married to a lawyer or an accountant or something like that."

"Yeah . . ." Wesley said thoughtfully. "With The Prince gone, you're the best now, right?"

"As far as they know."

"Okay, go to the fucking council. I'm going to hit his daughter."

"Why? What do you want to—?"

"I'll make it look like there's a gang of freaks after *all* of them. Make it so's they *have* to go after whoever's got a hard-on for them, you understand?"

"No."

"Look, they need to be fucking *scared*. I know how to do that. It's not just killing. When I'm done, they'll know it's no job for their foot soldiers. So that's when they'll turn it over to you."

"Depends. They could always—"

"An open contract's garbage, and you know it. How long was Gallo on the street? And Valachi? They only put out an open contract when it's not about them. And now they'll think it is."

"Nah, Wes. They really *wanted* Gallo."

"Sure, but for *money*, right? He wasn't coming into their fucking *houses* after them. It was just business with Gallo. This won't be. Not if they think that hitting The Prince turned his whole gang of psychos loose."

"So what? I still don't get this. If—"

"*You're* going to get them all together, Pet. You need to explain what they're up against, tell them what precautions to take. About this, they'll listen to you. When I get finished with this next one, they'll *all* show up to listen.

"And that's when we end this whole stupid fucking game of us working for them."

"You gonna play it so it looks like someone getting revenge for The Prince?"

"You're kidding me, right? Carmine taught me better than that. All those swine ever think about is throwing people like us away. If they think it's payback for The Prince, they'll just stake you out in that cesspool like a slab of beef waiting for the butcher."

"If not for The Prince, then . . ."

"This is gonna be like the freaks of the whole *world* rising up. They don't *need* a reason. It's going to be like those people opened a fucking box and the slime came squirming out over the rim."

"You can't . . ."

"It's not hard. I've been thinking about it. All I gotta do is be slick and *look* sick, that's all. Get me all the information on this woman. Make sure she's still there, get everything."

"Yeah, okay. But I don't—"

"Pet, this is the only way we can do it. The best chance we'll ever get."

Wesley went back to staring at the wall after Pet left, staring into it as if was a window, with vital information on the other side of the glass. He stayed there for three hours, not moving, breathing so shallowly that anyone watching might have thought him a battlefield casualty.

Finally, his eyes closed. He took a massive breath and got to his feet. Moving mechanically, he showered, shaved, and changed into a battered cord jacket and chinos. Sneakers and some black-rimmed glasses completed the student's outfit.

His next stop was the main library on 42nd Street. He stayed until it was near closing.

Two days later, Wesley drove up the FDR, heading north. It was just past noon when he found a parking place on East 51st, right near the river. He walked the rest of the way to Sutton Place, thinking of another 51st Street—in New York, the other side of the city was sometimes the other side of the world.

He found the address Pet had given him. The old man had told him that the security system was a joke— the people who lived in that neighborhood wanted the kind of classy building that wasn't bristling with electronic devices and rent-a-cops. But one *must* have a doorman. This one was a middle-aged clown who was dressed in the kind of uniform that self-respecting banana republics would have shunned, though it suited the kind of humans that dwelled in the building. Wesley took in the doorman's flat, expressionless face just before he sprang to open the door for a regal dowager. The doorman's flatness wasn't professional—he was just an ass-kisser who didn't waste his skills on non-members.

Wesley kept moving until he saw a sign saying that service deliveries were to be made in the rear. A glance down the narrow, super-clean little alley showed him that the service entrance wasn't guarded. But the sign telling tradesmen to ring the bell that was beneath it, was enough to tell him that it was kept locked. He returned to the car and drove back, thinking.

Pet was already inside the garage.

"You got everything?" Wesley asked.

"Yeah. Her husband works on The Street. Gets picked up every morning at eight sharp, but the return could be any time between seven-thirty and eleven.

"No dog. There's an intercom which lets her ring the doorman if she wants anything—so he can call a car service for her. She's got all those clubs and things, but she's home every Wednesday and Thursday morning for sure. They go out together couple of times a week, host parties in their place about once a month. No regular visitors. Getting in, that'll be the hard part."

"I'll have her father take me in."

Pet went back to polishing the Eldorado, not asking for explanations.

"That's the one I want for this," Wesley told him, nodding at the beige Caddy. "It already looks like someone rich owns it. Make it look like they take care of it, too."

Pet just nodded.

Wesley took a piece of paper out of his pocket, a news clipping.

"Pet, you know what they're talking about here?"

The old man quickly scanned the clipping and saw what Wesley wanted. "A letter bomb? Sure. It's no big thing. There's all kinds of fancy ones—mercury triggers, that kind of stuff. But all you really need is a spring that snaps when the mark opens the flap."

"Can you make one?"

"How big? Remember, the bigger the blast, the bigger the package."

"Big enough to blow someone up."

"One person? Sure."

"Inside of a regular letter?"

"If the envelope's heavy-enough paper."

"Rich people *always* write on heavy paper, right?"

"I guess," the old man said, dubiously.

"You see this column, the Debutante Ball? The third broad down on the line is DiVencenzo's daughter."

"So? He's nothing."

"But he can't do something like this without inviting the boss, right? So—the wife, she should be getting a whole bunch of invitations to stuff like this. That's why the weasels lay out so much coin . . . to get their daughters into the society columns."

"So?"

"So the boss's wife is gonna get a special invitation."

"How many of their women you gonna hit?"

"I think two will get it done. Starting at the top, right? If they don't, then we'll see. You get the stuff from outside; I'll meet you back here tonight. And get hold of the kid, too, okay?"

The three men sat in Wesley's apartment; the dog was on guard in the garage. Pet had assembled his materials on the workbench. Along with the spring-detonator and the grayish clay explosive charge, he had a package of 100-percent rag-content bond lilac paper. The matching envelopes were so stiff they resisted any attempt at bending. Their deep flaps held a discreetly fine-lined return address in a dark-purple italic script.

Dr. & Mrs. John I. Sloane III
Penthouse 2 • 708 Park Avenue
New York City, N.Y. 10021

Pet and the kid looked admiringly at the embossed calling cards.

"How come you didn't get the invitation printed, too, Wes?" the old man asked.

"Amy Vanderbilt says you always handwrite these things."

"Who?"

"In the library, Pet. There's not but one *correct* way to do these things."

"She'll never see the writing, anyway," the kid put in.

"That's not the point," Wesley replied. "What if they got an X-ray thing going, or something else we don't know about? Never take a risk you don't need to—that's how I was taught."

"Who's going to write the invitation?"

"None of *us* can do it, that's for sure."

The kid was studying the stationery. "I know an old woman who used to do this," he said.

"Go to these parties?"

"No, write these invitations. She's in a nursing home where they put me to work when I was on probation once. Those places they keep old people in, they're just like the joint. This lady used to make money addressing these things for some rich people—it was part of her job before the people she worked for said she got too old. Then she got dumped into that home. She's still there."

"How'd you know?"

"I go and see her every once in a while—she tells the other old people I'm her grandson. She used to sneak me extra food when I was on the cleaning crew there."

"She'll address this for you?"

"Sure."

Wesley looked at the kid. "After that, you got to leave her there."

"No! The fuck I do! They *already* left her there—she's already dead as far as everyone's concerned. She'd never rat me out."

"You sure?"

"I'm sure. She don't care about living anymore. She knows what's happening . . . what happened *to* her, I mean. I could fucking tell her *why* we was doing this and she'd be okay even then.

"Wesley, Mr. P., she *knows* I'm some kind of thief. She's old, but she's not slow. She's just doing time, and there's only one gate gonna ever open for her."

"What's she know about you?"

"Just what she thinks my name is, that's all. And that I give a fuck about her. She's not giving *that* up. Not for anyone. I know."

Wesley looked at Pet. The old man nodded: "When I was Upstate, the only people who you could ever count on visiting you was your mother, or your sister, or your grandmother. I ain't saying that's a woman thing—no big shock if your wife stopped coming—it's blood. What's she got to gain by giving the kid up? Besides, they're never going to find *that* envelope."

Wesley gave the kid several envelopes and some stationery. "Here's the address they get addressed to, okay?"

"Okay. I'll tell her that I found some work for her, get her to address a whole bunch of them. She wouldn't ever take money from me, but she'll do this. And she'll never know what's happening."

The kid went out the door alone. He was back in seconds. "Wes. That dog . . ."

"I know. Be right there."

Wesley stood in front of the three-panel mirror, rechecking. He had shaved extra carefully; Pet had given him an immaculate haircut and a professional manicure. On his left hand was a heavy white-gold wedding band, on his right a college ring: Georgetown University, 1960.

He wore a dark-gray summer-weight silk-and-mohair suit, a soft-green shirt with a spread collar, and a tiny-patterned gray tie with a moderate Windsor knot. He carried a slim attaché case, complete with combination lock and owner's monogram; the initials were "AS." Wesley checked his gold-cased watch; it was right on time.

The Eldorado looked as if it had been polished with beige oil, gleaming even in the dim light of the garage.

By nine-thirty that morning, Wesley was ostentatiously parking right in front of a fireplug on Sutton Place, well within the doorman's line of sight.

The doorman noted the El D with genuine approval. Too many of the high-class creeps in his building drove those foreign cars. He liked the looks of the guy getting out of the car, too. Calm and relaxed, not like those rush-rush snobs who breezed by him every day as if he didn't exist. Now, the way the guy parked that hog right in front of the plug and never looked back? That was *real* class.

Wesley smiled at the doorman. In spite of money, they were equals—two men who understood each other.

"Will you please ring the Benton suite? Tell them Mr. Salmone is here."

"Yes, sir!" snapped the doorman, pocketing Wesley's ten-dollar bill in the same motion.

The lady in 6-G asked the doorman to repeat the name a couple of times, then to describe the waiting man . . . and finally said to allow him up. Wesley walked past the doorman and into the lobby. The elevator cages were both empty. He stepped in, pushed the button, and rode to the sixth floor.

"What about the elevator operator?" Wesley had asked. Pet answered, "No sweat there. The cheap mother-fuckers fired them both a year ago. They said it was for efficiency, right? But they left a couple of old guys without a job. Probably without a pension, either."

Suite 6-G was all the way in the right-hand corner, just as the floor plan had shown. Wesley raised his hand to the bell, but the door was snatched open before he could make contact.

"Who are you?" the woman demanded.

"I'm from your father, Mrs. Benton."

"He knows better than this. I don't have anything to say to him."

"I only need five minutes of your time, Mrs. Benton. It's just some papers he wants you to sign."

"I thought I already did that years ago. How come he . . . ?"

"It will only take a moment," Wesley said, as he gently pushed the door open and stepped past her and into the apartment.

The place was quiet except for the raucous meow of a Persian cat reclining on the velvet sofa. Wesley walked toward the wall-length sofa as though he intended to sit down. The woman followed close behind him at a quicker pace, nervously patting her piled-up hair into place.

"Now, look! I told my father and I'll tell you, I—"

Wesley wheeled suddenly and slammed his right fist deep into the woman's stomach. She grunted and fell to the rug, retching. He slipped the brass knuckles off his hand and knelt beside the woman. She was struggling to breathe, her face a mottled mask of red and white. Wesley reached into his pocket and brought out a pair of anesthetic nose plugs. He inserted them into the woman's nostrils, put a handkerchief over her mouth, and watched closely until her breathing became slow and measured.

Satisfied she would stay unconscious for as long as the anesthetic lasted, he put on the surgeon's gloves, then carefully removed all his clothing, folding it neatly into the opened attaché case.

A thin stream of blood ran out of the corner of the woman's mouth—she must have bitten her lip.

Still didn't wake her up, ran through Wesley's mind as he laid the Beretta on the rug beside the woman, fitted the tube silencer, and doubled-locked the front door. The cat had vanished.

Pet had told him that the husband was a gourmet cook, so he knew what to look for.

He found the set of knives—hollow-ground Swedish steel with rosewood handles—and the portable butcher block on the stove island. He picked up the whole set and carried it back into the living room.

Wesley gently laid the woman's head on a couch pillow and placed the butcher block under her neck. When he pulled the pillow out from under her head and tugged back on her hair, the skin of her throat stretched taut, the veins in her neck leaping out against the pale skin.

He held the heavy butcher knife poised eighteen inches from her throat, mentally focused on a spot three inches beyond, and took a deep breath. The butcher knife flashed down. Blood spurted from her neck arteries. It took three more full-strength blows before the head came off completely.

Wesley grabbed the headless body by the ankles and dragged it toward the bedroom, leaving a thick trail of blood and paler fluids. He dumped the body on the bed and left the bedspread to absorb the mess while he went back for the head.

Wesley turned the body over on its back. He spread the woman's legs as far as they would go, quickly lashing her ankles to the legs of the matching teak bedposts with piano wire so they wouldn't close during rigor mortis. Then he took the head and pressed it down on the bed, moving it forward and backward in its own trail of fluid until it was slammed squarely between the woman's legs. Wesley used a tiny drop of Permabond to keep gravity from closing the eyes, leaving them staring straight ahead.

Next, he dug his right hand into the gaping neck and worked his fingers around until they were completely smeared with blood. He walked to the off-white wall behind the woman's body and used a finger to write:

> THE WAGES OF DEATH IS SIN!
> this is just beginning
> we know who you are
> we are coming for you
> you know who WE are

He went looking for the cat and found it under the rolltop desk in the den. Wesley pulled it out, careful at first so as not to be scratched, until he saw its claws had been removed, probably to protect the furniture. He stroked the animal to calm it down. And then pushed it into the den, closing the door behind him.

Wesley entered the Japanese-style bathroom and used a small screwdriver to remove the drain. Then he took a shower: first blazing hot, then icy cold. When he was completely clean and all the blood had vanished, he dried himself with a towel from his attaché case, leaving the water running.

Then he dressed, first putting the surgeon's gloves into a plastic bag and returning them to his case.

Before he left, he used the black silk handkerchief to wipe every surface. The library had told him that twelve points were necessary for a "true-positive" fingerprint ID, but five or more were "legally sufficient." His precaution was autopilot—Wesley knew if there was *any* identification at all, his case would never reach a courtroom.

Everything went back into the attaché case.

It was 10:56 when Wesley let himself out of the apartment, the handkerchief still in his hand as he turned the doorknob. The hallway was empty. He took the elevator downstairs, got off, and walked across the deserted lobby to the doorman.

The street was quiet. The sun was already boiling the concrete, but the people from that neighborhood went from their air-conditioned apartments to their air-conditioned cars to their air-conditioned offices. Nobody walked; they even paid people to walk their animals for them.

The doorman smiled at Wesley's approach. Wesley motioned him over.

"I have a package in my car for Mrs. Benton."

"Just bring it around to the back entrance, sir. The super will—"

"Mrs. Benton said she would like you to deliver this to her *personally*. Would that be all right?"

"Certainly, sir. If you'll just bring it inside here to me, I'll—"

"It's a little too big for that. Could I drive around to the service entrance and hand it to you there?"

"Yes, sir, you could, but I don't like to leave the door unattended."

"Mrs. Benton understands. She said to give you this for your trouble," Wesley said smoothly, handing the man a pair of twenty-dollar bills. "She doesn't want the package to leave your hands. Can you bring it right up to her?"

The doorman all but saluted. "I'll just wait here a couple of minutes to give you time to get around back—I don't want to be off my post too long."

"Appreciate it."

Wesley walked out the front door and climbed into the Eldorado. He drove off to the corner and turned right; the alley was only about eighty feet away. Wesley deliberately drove past the alley and then backed the big car down to the service entrance. He left the motor purring and quickly assembled the Beretta-and-silencer combo.

The service door opened in less than a minute. The doorman moved quickly toward the open window of Wesley's car, smiling. Wesley shot him twice in the chest. The impact was minimal; the doorman fell to the ground. Wesley opened his door, leaned out, and put three more slugs into the man's skull. He was out of the alley and driving along the side street in seconds.

Wesley drove crosstown without haste until he spotted a gray Fleetwood, just pulling out of a legal spot on Fifth Avenue as if it had been waiting for him.

He walked three blocks, then hailed a cab, which took him to the corner of Houston and Sullivan. A short hike down Sullivan toward Bleecker took him to Pet's Ford. As the Ford pulled away from the curb, the Fleetwood took its place.

The two men drove back toward the Slip. The kid hailed a cab to go pick up the Eldorado.

The headlines screamed

BIZARRE MURDER ON SUTTON PLACE!

The stories hinted at gruesome, unprintable details, but there were no photographs of the murder scene itself, and the basic facts didn't match the reality.

Wesley and Pet stayed in the building, waiting for the later editions. Amp-up time: MURDERED SOCIALITE WAS MAFIA CHIEFTAIN'S DAUGHTER! with the kind of follow-up "color" stories that humans like Salmone had come to hate ever since Colombo got himself veg-etablized for courting the press.

Pet was reading between the lines. "Christ, Wes, what'd you do to her?"

"It's better you don't know, right? You got to look surprised when they tell you about it. And if they polygraph this one, the murder method'll be one of the keys."

"You don't forget a thing anymore, huh?"

"I'll tell you what I *did* forget. I was going to fuck her when she was unconscious—or at least beat off onto the body. It'd freak them out even worse. I just forgot."

"Like fucking hell you 'forgot.' You couldn't do that, Wes—you're a man."

"I'm a bomb, old man," Wesley said, flatly. "And they lit my fuse a long time ago."

Wesley went out that night, leaving Pet behind. He drove the nondescript Ford up and down Allen Street. Whores approached the car at every light. It was quicker to look them directly in the face than to pretend to ignore them—they moved away the second they saw his eyes.

It took hours of prowling before he found what he wanted.

When he returned to the Slip, Pet was gone. The haphazard-appearing scrawls in the dust on the garage floor told Wesley the old man had gone to meet with his employers.

Wesley picked up the newspaper Pet had left behind for him. Page three had a story about a letter bomb that had exploded in the face of Nancy Jane DiVencenzo of Long Island's tony North Shore. The police had no clue to the sender—the letter had been blown into microscopic particles, along with the young deb's face.

Wesley went to his own place and let himself in. He took the dog up to the top floor and let it run free on the hardwood for an hour while he focused on the white wall. The dog alternatively loped and turned on vicious bursts of speed; he kept at it until Wesley drew a deep breath and sat up. They went down to the apartment together, the dog taking the point, as always.

The soft, insistent buzzing woke Wesley at 3:25 in the morning, telling him the old man was back. He dressed and went down to the basement garage.

The dog acknowledged his passage with a throaty growl, and Wesley realized that he had never seen the animal sleep.

The old man was smoking one of the black, twisted cigars he liked. He almost never did this inside the garage. The exhaust fan was running like Vaseline flowing through oil, so silent it could only be sensed, not heard.

"You got them, Wes—you got them *all*. I almost threw up behind just *hearing* about it. The woman's husband is in Bellevue. He's never gonna be right. They can't agree on much, but they know some sicko crew's after them all. The Long Island guy got the phone call in the middle of last night—he was already in the city for a meet on the Sutton Place thing. He went fucking crazy. They tied it in, just like we expected."

"The cops—"

"The honest ones're probably laughing. What the fuck do they care? But they all know the sky's the limit for any real info."

"Leads?"

"Forget it. The big man himself said it had to be a fucking ghost what done it."

"It was."

"I know. I used to light candles for Carmine, Wes. But I finally realized that it was just another club he couldn't join."

"What'd you tell them?"

"I told them it had to be a freak from the cesspool. I said I'd hit the area and nose around until I came up with something, put a lot of my people on the street, all that bullshit. Then I gave them a whole bunch of crap about the security arrangements they'd need for their families. Like we said, right?"

"Perfect. I found a building. On Chrystie, south of Delancey, on the west side of the block. The whole building's empty—three stories. It's got buildings on either side, both higher, both abandoned."

"Abandoned, my ass. You got people squatting in every fucking X-flat in this city."

"That's no problem. They don't see nothing going in. And, going out, there won't be nothing left *to* see. Let's look tomorrow night."

Wesley went all the way up to the roof and sat, smoking as he looked at the Manhattan Bridge. He and Pet had stockpiled enough explosives to lift the building he'd found on Chrystie into orbit—it wouldn't be difficult to completely mine the place and set it off with a radio control. But there was just no way that Pet could excuse himself and leave the room, much less the building, not with those kinds of humans inside and all mega-tense like they'd be.

Risk against gain. Wesley sat and thought about

some political pamphlet he'd read in prison. Lee had given it to him. Everyone respected Lee for being in the know, but the pamphlet had never made sense to Wesley. How could the writer talk about the lumpen proletariat being the vanguard of the revolution when the fucking lumpen proletariat couldn't even understand the fancy-ass words the man used in a book they'd never read? Or was that a criticism of Marx by some *other* fucking lame who thought the lumpen were terrific? Lee read those tracts like they were comic books—he kept chuckling over them. Nobody ever understood what he was laughing about, and he never explained.

"An ox for the people to ride . . ." Who wanted to be a fucking ox? Work all your life and then have them eat your flesh when you're too old to work or breed. The prison-reform freaks had it all wrong. Wesley remembered when the cons threatened to riot behind their demand for conjugal visiting, and Lee told them they had conjugal visits in Mississippi, where he'd done time before. Wesley asked him why *Mississippi*, of all places, would treat prisoners so good.

"Because the cons down there, they ain't nothing but motherfucking work animals. You feed them and you keep them serviced, or they turn mean and lazy on you. Prisons is a big business down there, Wes," Lee told him. "Chopping cotton, same way we did when they first brought us over. Don't cost the taxpayers a dime—the prisons *make* money for the State."

Wesley thought about the plate shop and all the bogus dealer-plates the cons made for sale to the guards, who, in turn, sold them to the mob and used the money to buy dope to sell back to the cons, who stabbed each other to death over the distribution rights and ended up locked in solitary, watched by those same guards.

He remembered another contribution from Lee's library: Mao's "The guerrilla is the fish in the water; the leaf on the tree." And remembered how he'd thought you had to be a damn slimy fish to swim in this city.

Finally, he faced it. Wiping out Carmine's employers wouldn't end it. He couldn't let Pet go just for that. Wesley was deep into his second pack of cigarettes when he got to his feet to go downstairs. It was nearly dawn, and the street was starting to lighten, but it was still as deserted as ever.

It would have to be gas.

The next night, the two men looked over the building. It was easy enough to get into the back once Pet torched off the bolts. He replaced them with his own, adding fresh locks for which he had good keys.

When they got to the top floor, Wesley asked, "Can you make this room airtight?"

"In a couple of weeks, sure. But we won't be able to do it quietly."

"Have we got enough to buy this building?"

"Yeah, but if you're going to leave them all here . . ."

"Buy it in Carmine's name."

"Come *on*, Wes. Be yourself. We need only clean paper on something like this."

"Can you get that?"

"Sure. For about ten large, from the Jew on Broome Street."

"I heard of him, but I don't know where he is, exactly. Do you?"

"No, but I can find him easy enough. He's a professional."

"Okay. Try it that way first. Buy the building and get us all the stuff we talked about."

"I don't think you should work on that part, Wes. Let me use the kid—it's really only a two-man job, anyway."

They found the kid inside the garage, sitting next to the Ford. The dog was standing by the entrance to Wesley's hallway, watching; he sat down when Wesley came in. The kid looked at the floor.

"The old lady's dead," he said.

"What old lady?" Wesley asked him.

"The lady who addressed the envelopes for us, remember?"

"Yeah. You had to . . . ?"

"I called for her this morning, and they told me she killed herself last night. Took about fifty sleeping pills. She must've been saving them for weeks."

"You think she knew?"

"Yeah, she knew, all right. She was old, not stupid. I told you she'd never give me up."

Pet put his hand on the kid's shoulder. "I never thought she would, kid. She loved you. So she had to make sure they'd never come for you through her."

The kid nodded.

Wesley never changed expression. He abandoned his plans to visit the old lady, snapped his fingers for the dog, and went to his apartment, leaving Pet and the kid alone to plan the building project.

Wesley spent the next five days on the top floor, the next four nights on the roof. He read the papers carefully, as he always did. The news carried a column about a new methadone clinic being opened up on Pike Street. It was directly across from the Projects and only about six blocks away from the factory on Water Street. Wesley felt an overpowering sense of encroachment, as if a malevolent force had just entered his life.

He went back into his newspaper file. The headlines formed a story sequence on their own:

ADDICTS OVERRUN RESIDENTIAL COMMUNITY

CITIZENS UP IN ARMS OVER NEW
METHADONE CLINIC

ARRESTS TRIPLE NEAR NEW CLINIC

CITIZENS' COMMITTEE REPORTS ALL
RESIDENTS LIVE IN FEAR

COMMUNITY GROUP COMPLAINS OF
LOWERED PROPERTY VALUES

VIGILANTES THREATEN TO BURN NEW
METHADONE CENTER

Wesley reflected, deep within himself. Cocaine was going way up in price. Methadone didn't block reaction to Lady Snow, the way it did with heroin. Girl had more kick than Boy, and Freebase was the coming thing. Carmine had told him, hundreds of times, that no government policy was ever an accident, but this . . .

Methadone. A way to register every dope fiend in the country. A way to control habits, supplies, prices . . . lives.

Wesley thumbed through the laboriously titled "Methadone Maintenance Treatment Program of the New York City Health Services Administration: Policy and Procedure Manual," and finally found what he was looking for on page E-1:

> *"Although the Program does not consider detoxification as the ultimate goal that defines 'success,' some patients do see this as their own, personal objective. . . ."*

Wesley had asked the librarian for any official publications on the program, but was bluntly told such information was not public. Three days later, a junkie had met Wesley in front of the Felt Forum and gotten into the Ford.

"I got it, man," he had said, handing over the manual. "You got the bread?"

"Yeah," Wesley told him, tucking the bills into the junkie's shirt pocket. "You want to make another fast hundred?"

"Sure, man. I need—"

"I know. Just hang on, now."

Wesley swung the car into the Eighth Avenue traffic stream and took Eighth all the way to 57th. From there, he went crosstown and got on the upper roadway of the 59th Street Bridge. They crossed the bridge in silence, the junkie unaware they were bracketed by Pet in the cab and the kid in the Fleetwood.

Carmine had told him, "You ever go to a meet with a junkie, you remember two things: one, go with cover; and two, *don't* go heeled. Every fucking junkie is a potential rat, and an ex-con, packing, in *this* state, you're down for the whole count."

The junkie was already nodding off the free cap Wesley had laid on him—his tolerance was for heroin, not Thorazine. He was drifting into unconsciousness as Wesley parked on the bridge between Northern Boulevard and Skillman Avenue in Long Island City, overlooking Sunnyside Yard. The yard was once the world's biggest railroad center, but it was largely abandoned now. The only business the neighborhood did was the giant Queens Social Services Center—the city's new euphemism for "Welfare"—on the corner.

Wesley hauled the junkie out of the car. He leaned himself and the junkie against the railing. The street was empty. A cab cruised by slowly, Pet at the wheel. The junkie was barely breathing. Wesley had read about people so relaxed that they didn't die even when falling from great heights. He slammed the ice pick into the back of the junkie's neck and shoved him over the railing in one smooth motion.

A big red-white-and-blue sign materialized on Water Street, right across from the factory. It proclaimed

the area to be part of the TWO BRIDGES RECLAMA-
TION PROJECT. Wesley figured that the only thing
"reclaimed" would be the fixer's piece of the federal
expenditures, and that nothing would be torn down or
built there for years. Plenty of time.

But a methadone clinic, that was another story
entirely—too close and too much trouble.

Methadone meant government-inspected dope. It
meant sales-and-service. And too many greedy people
always sliding around in their own grease.

Pet came back later in the day. He told Wesley that
the building on Chrystie had been purchased—he and
the kid were going to get to work on it right away.

Wesley just nodded, deep in his own problems.

The triplex pump was installed without difficulty. It
would work to almost unlimited pressures and func-
tion for more than sixteen hours straight at top speed.
The pump was connected to a simple tubing system
with seventy-two tiny outlets bored into the ceiling.
The hydrocyanic acid was easy to obtain. When forced
through alcohol, it produced a gas much more deadly
than the apple-blossom perfume they used to snuff
enemies of the state in California.

The interior rapidly took shape: expensive leather
lounge chairs, a wet bar against one wall, a huge blackboard directly opposite, indirect lighting, a highly polished hardwood floor, a large air-conditioning unit
prominently displayed in the single window.

The marks wouldn't be remotely suspicious of bars

across the windows of any building being renovated in that part of town. The entrance to the room was only through a pocket door. But instead of the usual four-inch penetration, this door went two feet into the frame, activating a series of snap locks with every six inches it moved down its track.

Wesley and Pet went over the plans dozens of times; revised them again and again; discussed, modified, refined, changed, sharpened, rejected . . . always polishing. The kid was going to have to be used for this one, too. There wasn't any other way, and they'd be short-handed as it was.

"Remember, unless everything goes *exactly* like we expect, the whole thing is off."

"Wes, maybe we'll never get another chance," Pet said. "So what if we . . . ?"

"Forget it. There's a lot more to do now. Stuff I didn't know about before. This is for Carmine, but there's a lot left for me and you, after."

"I don't get it. I thought we were just going to take them and—"

"We are, but I'm not going with them. And . . . and you're not, either, Pet."

"Okay," the old man said slowly. "Only if everything goes perfect."

Tuesday, 10:33 p.m. Pet's cab pulled up at the back-alley door to the building on Chrystie Street. The ill-tempered don in the back seat said, "I still don't see why we couldn't bring our own cars."

"It's security, Mr. G. This way, you have your own bodyguard with you, but if those freaks are watching your home, they'll think you're still there. And they'd never try anything like that on your kids if you *was* home, right?"

The don didn't answer, but grunted in agreement.

He waited in the car while Pet rapped three times sharply on the steel slab. The kid opened the door. He wore a shoulder holster filled with a .45 and carried an M3 grease gun with the stock fully retracted. He saluted Pet, who waved the two waiting men inside.

The kid said, "Please be seated and make your-selves comfortable, gentlemen. The others will be arriv-ing shortly." The first-floor room was soundproofed. A large-screen color TV took up most of the space in one corner. "If you want a drink or something to eat, or any-thing at all," the kid said, "just ask me, okay?"

By 11:45 p.m., they were all assembled. Salmone had been the last to arrive, as befitted his station in the hierarchy. The kid went outside, changed places with Pet, and drove off in the cab.

Inside, Pet addressed the assembled group. "Gentle-men! We are going upstairs to a room where we can talk and where I can show you the things I've discovered about these freaks. They can be hit; but it's going to cost—"

Mumbled chorus of:

"Naturally."

"Who gives a fuck?"

"*Whatever* it costs!"

"—and I have to insist that, for your own protection,

I be the only one to talk when we're upstairs," Pet continued. "That way there won't be any need to waste time searching for bugs. You can put your own bodyguards anyplace around the building or inside that you want, but be sure they can't be seen."

Salmone immediately took over. "Tony, over here. You and Sal stay by this back door; Johnny, come upstairs with me. Okay? Lenny, have your man take the front door with Sam's guy. Al, you leave a couple of men on the stairs. I need at least two more men outside the upstairs door. Everybody else, come with us."

The men moved silently into position. Pet led the way upstairs. They all filed into the big room. The door slid closed behind them so quietly that it was impossible to judge the depth to which it penetrated into the panel. The air conditioner was the only sound in the room.

Pet walked to the front of the room and seated himself behind a small desk in front of the blackboard. The others arranged themselves in a loose semicircle facing him, the bosses seated and the bodyguards standing. There was no hum of conversation—snapping fingers and impatient gestures indicated desires for drinks, cigars to be lighted, and deployment of personnel.

Pet began to talk. "We got the whole story now. It's a whole fucking crew of freaks. Longhairs. All on drugs. They call themselves the People's Harvest of Vengeance, and they got connections to the . . ."

As Pet was talking, the kid approached the two men standing outside the back door in the alley. He showed himself clearly, hands spread in the reflected light so the men would relax. There was no sound, but the top of one guard's head seemed to mushroom from under his hat—he fell heavily to the ground. The kid immediately glanced up toward the roof; the other guard involuntarily followed with his own eyes. The kid was already bringing up his own silenced pistol—the slug caught the second guard full in the chest, killing on contact.

The kid whistled sharply, craning his neck to throw the sound up to where Wesley knelt on the roof, holding the silenced M16. As the kid pocketed his own weapon, Wesley gently tossed the rifle over the edge of the roof; it sailed flat through the air and into the kid's arms. Practicing that maneuver to perfection-certainty had been a bitch.

The kid quickly laid down the rifle and opened the back door. Then he dragged the dead men inside. Taking the rifle, he walked quickly through the building until he came to a blank wall. He pulled a lever, and a portion of the wall slid out. The kid stepped through the opening and kept walking, until he was near the front of the building, facing the street.

There was no glass in the big front window, and the backs of the two guards were clearly visible. Secure they were covered, they focused all their attention on the street. They were taking their job seriously—unlike the cash, the fear that gripped their bosses had trickled *all* the way down.

The kid found the three-foot tripod and felt around in the dark until he located the three mounting holes Pet had drilled deep into the concrete. He assembled the tripod and jammed it into the holes, attached the rifle, and sighted along the barrel. There was more than enough light to see by.

The kid held the rifle steady on the back of the guard to his left, then swung it to his right toward the spine of the second man. He did this several times, then adjusted the socket under the tripod's head so that the rifle stopped dead at the place where he would sight the second man. He tested the socket by slamming the rifle hard to the right—it held, solid and silent.

The rifle was sighted into the spine of the first guard, just above his waist. Both men were roughly the same height, so it was even easier than they had planned— the kid only had to adjust for lateral movement. He focused hard until the first guard's back was the only thing in his vision, then slowly squeezed the trigger. As the first guard slumped, the kid slammed the rifle hard to the right, simultaneously pulling the trigger so that the shot came when the barrel was pointing directly at the second guard.

The kid checked to be sure the street was quiet, then he began to drag the bodies inside. A faint rustling from the shadows sent him springing cat-footed into the alley. On autopilot, he slammed his knife between the ribs of a wino who'd made the error of stirring in his alcoholic sleep.

Wesley crawled from the roof into what was once a ventilation shaft, holding the Doberman on a short lead. When they reached the corridor leading to the top floor, Wesley could just make out the two men. They were standing alertly, listening for any sound, not talking. And clearly visible to the dog. Wesley unsnapped the lead.

The Doberman shot down the corridor, as quiet as cancer, its claws never slipping on the roughened floor; it hit the nearest guard like a ninety-pound razor blade and dropped him silently to the ground. The other guard whirled. He screamed once before the silenced Beretta took him down. The dog ripped out the first guard's throat and flew down the stairs. His charge carried both men coming up the stairs back down—they all tumbled to the second floor, landing in a mess of blood and screams. The kid was working his way up the stairs with a machete, hacking a path toward Wesley, who had switched to a similar weapon.

It was over in seconds. The place was as silent as the tomb it had become. Not a sound penetrated the upstairs chamber where Pet was holding forth.

Wesley snapped "Stay!" at the now calm dog, and sprang over the bodies to the first floor. He took out a plastic box about the size of a pack of cigarettes and flipped the single tiny toggle switch. A red light flashed on Pet's desk, readily visible to most of the assembled men.

"Relax!" Pet called out. "That just means we're giving off too much static electricity and we could get monitored. I'm going to spray this stuff on the floor around your chairs—it'll just take a second. Remember: please don't move."

Pet walked into the midst of the mobsters. When he reached the back wall near the bar, he began to spray a heavy silicon mixture all over the floor, always being careful, although not obviously so, to spray the area he had just vacated. He seemed to run out of spray when he got to his own area, and took another can off his desk to continue. The whole operation took less than a minute. When he was finished, he pushed a wide, flat button under his desk with his knee and quickly resumed speaking:

"So, like I said, the scumbags can be wasted, but it's got to be in Times Square, where they hole up. I'll need at least twenty soldiers. *Good* ones. It's going to splash all over the papers. I know that's not what you *want*, but there's no choice, not anymore. Those hippies are psycho, and they'll rip up every one of your . . ."

The hissing of the hidden jets was masked by the hum of the air conditioner. Cyanide is colorless, but the dim lighting masked even the slight air movement.

After about ten seconds, Salmone took a deep breath and hissed, "Gas!" He leaped from his chair toward the door and fell flat on his face—the surface was as slippery as Teflon. One of the bodyguards clawed his way to a window and battered it frantically with his gun butt; the bars held firm. The fattest don swam his way through the grease to the door; it held against the full magazine in his pistol.

Within another five seconds, all the men in the room were on their knees or flattened. Only Salmone remembered what he had lived for. He held his breath and carefully leveled his fallen bodyguard's pistol at where Pet had been, but the old man was as safe behind the steel-lined desk as he would have been outside the room.

The door popped open. Wesley and the kid stepped through the slot, wearing gas masks with oxygen backpacks. They skidded over to Pet, and then got a good grip—his part of the floor wasn't slippery. The kid pulled

Pet toward the door and closed it behind him, leaving Wesley inside. He slapped the portable oxygen mask onto the old man's face and started the compressor. Pet still had a feeble pulse, but his skin was bluish and bloated. Wesley knew you could beat cyanosis with oxygen and adrenaline. The kid found the vein in the old man's arm, slapped on the Velcro tourniquet, and pumped in five cc's.

Inside the room, Wesley was hacking his way through tons of flesh with the machete as the triplex continued to pump its deadly fumes. It took him almost five minutes to be sure he got the job done. He pounded three times on the door. It opened enough to show the kid, holding the grease gun. Wesley held up his left fist, and the kid slid the door the rest of the way open. Wesley stepped out. The old man was already sitting up.

"I fucking forgot to hold my breath after I hit the fucking switch. . . . How the fuck could I . . . ?"

"Shut up!" the kid told him angrily.

Wesley and the kid carried the old man downstairs. When they got to the first floor, Wesley and the old man sat down to wait until the kid returned with the car. Wesley said "Guard!" to the Doberman and went all the way back upstairs to the big room.

He shut off the pump and reconnected it to another tank. He threw the switch again, and the triplex started throwing raw gasoline all over the building at two hundred gallons per minute. Wesley took a mass of putty-colored substance out of a plastic pouch and carefully molded it to the side of the pump, running a thin trail of the same stuff to a wooden box about ten feet away.

The place reeked of gasoline by the time Wesley got

downstairs. The kid pulled into the alley with the car, and they gently laid Pet across the back seat. The old man struggled and, with a powerful effort, pulled himself erect. The dog got into the back with him and lay down on the floor.

At 1:20 a.m., the Ford turned down Houston, heading for the East River. Wesley reached for the switch on the radio transmitter. Before he touched it, he felt the old man's gnarled hand on his. He looked back at the darkness in the back seat for a second. Then they threw the switch, together.

As the car slowed for a light on Houston, the sky above Chrystie fired to a brilliant orange-red. The car purred east.

For the first time, the kid came inside the garage with them to stay. The old man was able to reach his bed by himself. The kid slept right beside him.

Wesley and the dog went to their apartment. In minutes, they were all asleep.

The *News* said the fire had claimed the lives of "at least thirty-one people," and had caused another eleven to be hospitalized. The authorities were strongly divided as to the cause of the homicidal arson. They sifted the ruins meticulously. If they found anything besides miscellaneous flesh and bone, it never made the papers.

Minor wars soon erupted among mob factions throughout the city, eastern Long Island, and northern New Jersey. They quickly escalated, and bigger people were called in from outside to settle things.

Paranoia was running wild, and everyone was so busy distrusting and plotting that even those who knew who had been at the meeting never thought to look for Petraglia. It was assumed he died in the blaze with the others.

A voodoo church that had been meeting in a cellar under one of the movie houses in Times Square was dynamited, with four people killed. The police had more informers than they could pay.

Crackdowns on drunks took place from one end of the Bowery to the other. The law said it was okay to be a drunk, but being a flaming menace to society was something else.

It was popularly assumed that a wino had fallen asleep with a lit cigarette until some bright boy leaked the identity of the bodies inside the building. The columnists had a field day, but nothing compared to the florists—they hadn't done such lavish, cost-no-account displays since Dion O'Banion was doing that kind of work.

Wesley worked days on his project. The compounding was easy enough—a four-to-one mixture of ammonium nitrate and TNT produces a good facsimile of Amatol, the best military-industrial explosive for large-scale demolition work. He made the mercury-fulminate detonators himself, packing each one inside a sealed aluminum tube about the size of a mechanical pencil. The explosives were hermetically sealed inside zinc boxes, then packed into wooden crates. Pet had drilled each of the boxes so that the mercury-fulminate pencils snapped into position instantly.

Nights, Wesley spent on the roof. Alone. There was a lot to think about. But first the area had to be clean. There were already too many cops around during the day. Junkies were a magnetic force field: if you couldn't find a dealer to shake down, you could always justify your shift by hauling in a few users. Even simple possession could be upgraded to a felony collar; law enforcement courted raw numbers more intensely than any CPA.

Wesley finally admitted to himself that he had expected Pet to check himself out in the gas chamber they had built. But he hadn't let the old man go, and he wasn't sure why.

He waited patiently until the rehab of the building on Pike Street was nearly complete. Then he and the kid went to the site in broad daylight, each carrying two of the wooden crates. He had made the kid practice until he could handle thirty-five pounds on each shoulder like it wasn't much of anything. The crates were clearly marked GENERATOR PARTS: THIS SIDE UP! and they had no trouble placing one in each corner of the top floor.

They repeated the same exact move several more times, until there were twenty boxes of the mixture in place.

The last night, they returned again—this time with the Doberman. They left the dog near the door and went downstairs. The place was ready-made for junkies, all right—as easy to break into as a glass vault. They planted sixty sticks of fuseless dynamite in the basement. Harmless without blasting caps . . . unless there was a massive explosion in the immediate vicinity.

On the top floor, Wesley rigged a magnesium fuse from each of the fulminate-of-mercury pencils. Then he and the kid walked backward, both hands full of the trailed fuse wires. They met in the center of the empty floor, forming a giant spider's web.

As they went down the back stairs with the dog, Wesley reflected that it wasn't much use writing slogans on a wall if you planned to total the building. The tiny propane torch had been placed with its tip pointing into the middle of the spider's web. The hard part had been the trip mechanism, but the salesman at Willoughby-Peerless had been only too happy to demonstrate how the motor-driven Nikon F could be activated at distances up to a full mile with a radio transmitter, especially when he spotted Wesley for the kind of chump who would pay retail. The whole tab came to over three grand, and the salesman went home happy. Wesley went home with exactly what *he* wanted, too.

That night, he and the kid set up the Nikon so that its mirror mechanism flipped the series-wired little torches into action. Then they closed the door behind them, and Wesley smeared several tubes of the epoxy back and forth across the seams which they had hand-sanded to the smoothness of glass. Thanks to Hobart Chan, they already knew that a single drop would hold a car door shut against a man trying desperately to get out—what they applied would hold against anything short of an explosion. They stuck the aluminum sign with its skull-and-crossbones in black on a white background on the door and left. In bright-red lettering, it said:

KEEP OUT! DANGER!
POISON GAS USED FOR EXTERMINATION!

The papers promised a "gala event" at the new methadone clinic. All the public supporters of methadone maintenance—actors, politicians, anyone wealthy or famous enough to rate a photo—would be hosted to a superb lunch prepared by the addicts themselves. It was widely hailed by the *Times* as:

> *. . . one of the few issues around which New York-ers remain united. In spite of dissident factions which oppose methadone clinics, those with a vision for this city recognize that methadone maintenance programs are a necessary element in the fight against narcotics addiction. The clinics are here to stay.*

The gala was scheduled for noon on Thursday, a slow news day. Extensive press coverage was expected.

Thursday, 12:35 p.m. The newly christened Methadone Maintenance Center was open for business and playing to a packed house. In an attempt to "involve the community," as the *Times* duly reported, the doors had been thrown open to the public. The chance to mingle with all the celebrities was too good to pass up—mothers brought their children, housewives drove in from far-flung suburbs, and physicians with no more interest in narcotics-control than in socialized medicine flocked to the center.

Wesley took the radio transmitter to the roof on the Slip to minimize signal interference, as the helpful salesman had suggested. He went up alone: there was a tacit agreement between Wesley and the old man that he would be the only one to go up on the roof.

The range was right—but if it didn't fire, he'd just have to move it closer. Wesley pressed the switch. There was a dead silence in his head. He mentally counted backward from one hundred, like the time they'd operated on his leg in the Army and they had pumped the Sodium Pentothal into him.

He was all the way down to eighty-eight when a dull, booming roar rose out of Pike Street and swept across town toward the river in thundering waves. A much larger explosion followed—the sound deeper, resonating at a different harmonic. All the sounds that followed were indistinguishable from the general madness that engulfed every noise within it.

Surviving spectators said that the roof of the building had literally jumped into the air. Then the entire front of the building had simply vanished in smoke. TV programs were interrupted with horror-struck announcers saying there was nothing but rubble where the center had been. Seven different precincts responded to the fire calls. Squad cars stopped all traffic on the street until well past dark.

A roving reporter interviewed a long-haired young man just back from gunner duty on a helicopter in Vietnam; he asked if the young man had ever seen anything like that before. The machine-gunner just shrugged: "Sure. There's more bodies here, that's all."

The papers were full of estimated body counts, and the FBI was invited to participate in the case by an anguished mayor. In spite of the fire trucks, the ruins smoldered for several days—water pressure was low in the area, because of all the open hydrants. The blast had blown several buildings completely apart and had thrown death-dealing chunks of concrete and steel as far as a hundred yards. One hundred and nine individuals were known dead by the third day of counting, with identification of some not yet complete.

The mayor dismissed persistent rumors that the bombing was the work of some group opposed to a methadone clinic in their neighborhood. "There have been minor incidents elsewhere, but the people of my city know they can always get a redress of their grievances at City Hall."

The *News*'s "Inquiring Photographer" did a street survey on reactions to the explosion. The results were never printed.

At least six political groups anonymously claimed credit for the bombing, calling it everything from "bringing imperialistic war home to the pigs," to "a manifesto written in dynamite." None was taken too seriously by anyone but the FBI, which was already counting the increased budget appropriations.

Every columnist had his favorite candidate, although

"terrorists" remained the front-runner. Rumors of a cult surfaced occasionally, but never gained much momentum.

There was a mass funeral for the "methadone victims." Many of the families of the dead declined the privilege.

Wesley returned to the roof to think.

Seeing that the old man didn't want to talk, Wesley walked through the garage and into his own area. The Mansfield job was the first they had done strictly for the money. Their employers were fundamentally unchanged despite recent events—regrouped, cautious, but with the same limited ways of carving out their unique monopolies. Because they thought the old man died in the gas attack, Wesley negotiated with them directly.

He had handled the Mansfield negotiations just like Carmine had taught him: No questions, just a price. Half up front, with the rest on completion. The people who ordered his death were the kind of men who routinely substituted their paranoia for proof.

Wesley stripped off all the clothing he had worn on the job and stuffed it into a large paper bag. The jewelry came off, too, to be filed with hundreds of similar articles. The incinerator would later claim all the clothing—part of the cost of doing business.

After a quick shower, Wesley dressed again and headed for the firing range on the fourth floor. He carefully sighted in and calibrated the new M16s Pet had bought from a warrant officer at Fort Dix. A few missing guns from the overall inventory were automatically charged against the manufacturer, who was, in turn, building the guns so far below the specifications agreed to in the government contract that protesting the slight extra charge was unthinkable.

Wesley was able to obtain all the military ordnance he wanted, and everyone's illusions were preserved . . . even down to the two boots who thought they were delivering the M16s to a government agent who was going to run a "spot check" to make sure they worked well enough to protect our boys in whatever jungle they would be fighting in that year.

Wesley always disassembled each weapon and rebuilt it to the correct specs, using the manual as a guide. He remembered throwing away his own rifle in Korea when he finally got his hands on a solid, reliable Russian AK-47—nobody in his outfit was carrying Army-issue by then. They all had sidearms, which were supposed to be only for officers. They threw away the cumbersome grenade-launchers ("Lost in combat, sir!") and even copped the Russian knives when they could loot a body unobserved.

Something about all that had puzzled Wesley, and he finally decided to ask the smartest guy in the outfit about it. Morty was a short, wiry-haired Brooklyn boy who always had his face in a book.

"They want us to win this war, right?"

"This isn't a war, Wes. It's a police action."

"When the police go into action in my neighborhood, it *is* war."

"What I mean is, Congress hasn't declared war on the North Koreans," Morty explained, patiently. "It's the United Nations that's doing this."

"It's the North Koreans against the South Koreans, right?"

"So . . . ?"

"So why don't we let them settle their own beef?"

"Because of Communism, Wes. The North Koreans are controlled by the Reds, and they want to take over the whole fucking world. If we don't stop them here, we'll have to fight them in America eventually."

"And we own the South Koreans, right?"

"No. Nobody 'owns' them. What the South Koreans want is to be free."

"So why don't they fight?"

"They *do* fight. It's just that—"

"Oh, bullshit, man. They don't do shit but rip us off. They let their women be diseased whores, and they wash the fucking dishes and do the laundry and all. . . . I mean, why don't they fight *us*?"

"We're on their side—we're helping them get free."

"A zip's a zip, right? That's what everyone says—once we start blasting, everything yellow goes down."

"Yeah. Well, look . . . why did you ask me if we want to win?"

"If we want to win, why'd they give us such lousy guns?"

"Well, you know the factories. In wartime, speed counts, so they have to—"

"I thought this was a fucking police action."

"Man, Wes, you get harder and harder to talk to."

"You know what I think, Morty?"

"What?"

"I think *we're* the bullets, you know?"

Wesley went back to reloading some new cartridge casings. He finished at about 3:00 a.m. and climbed up to the roof. He was dressed in double-knit black jersey pants and shirt. Socks of the same material went almost to the knee. He wore mid-calf leather boots which closed with Velcro fasteners. The boots had been worked for hours with Connolly's Hide Food until they were glove-soft, and the crosscut crepe soles gave superb traction without making a sound. He had on a soft, black felt hat—with the jersey's turtleneck, it made an unbroken line of black to anyone behind him. Dark-gray deerskin gloves hid his hands. The same black paste that football players use to protect their eyes from reflected glare was smeared across both cheekbones and the bridge of his nose.

In the roof's blackness he was just another shadow.

Wesley put the night glasses to his face and dispassionately watched a gang of car-strippers at work under the only remaining streetlight in the area, about two blocks north of Pike Slip. Unlike the junkies, these kids were anxious to avoid contact with the rest of the human race while they were working. They were the same as the birds in the trees in Korea had been—everything was safe as long as you saw them, or heard them going about their business.

The old man worried him. Pet had tried to check out in the gas chamber. They both knew this, and it changed the way they did business. Pet couldn't hit the street at all anymore—Wesley had to rely on the kid.

They were working only for money now. Before they put all of Carmine's old enemies in the gas chamber, Wesley hadn't thought about the future. He was out of prison with a job to do. Nothing but a guided missile. But now he was a missile that hadn't exploded when it had connected with its target. Empty. He had to think about "tomorrow" now, and it was a new experience.

Wesley climbed down the stairs. Before he went back to his own apartment, he checked the garage. The old man had a blank look on his face, polishing the cars for the hundredth time. They gleamed like jewels, *too* bright for work.

The next morning, the old man was polishing the Ford as Wesley slipped into the garage. For the first time, the old man hadn't turned when someone entered. Wesley walked up to the Ford and just stared silently until the old man finally turned to face him.

"What?"

"I want to talk to you, Pet. You want to check out of here?"

"Yeah. I wanted to check out when I had to do that Prince motherfucker . . . and you knew it and you wouldn't let me. And that was good, Wes. The right thing. But you should have left me in that room there on Chrystie."

"I know it. I know it *now*, anyway."

"I waited for you, for Carmine's son, all those fucking years because I had a *reason*, you know? We'd either get all of them or they'd get us. Or both. All the same, right? That was all there was. All I care about was in that room. I can't even *drive* anymore, you know what I'm saying?"

"I know, Pet. But . . ."

"There ain't no 'but' behind this, Wes. If I get spotted now, they'll hit me. And what's worse, they'll fucking know I was involved in that gas job. They'll know there was other people. They'll know, and they'll smell around, and sooner or later . . ."

"I know."

"I was going to go out *hard*, you know? Take some of them with me. But there's none of them really left. Except maybe a few new guys we couldn't ever get close to. And the soldiers, the button men, you know how that works. You kill one, they get another."

"No soldier's going to hit you, Pet."

"It wouldn't be right. I helped kill the sharks, Wes—I don't want the fucking little minnows to nibble my flesh. I'm tired. . . ."

"Your family . . . ?"

"Gone. A long time ago. Carmine was my family, and then you."

"I still am."

"Then *be* family, Wesley."

"That's why I came down here."

"Yeah. What was your mother's name?" the old man challenged.

"I don't know."

"Did you learn enough from me to be proud of that?"

"I did, Pet."

"I want to stay here, right?"

"I wasn't thinking about no Potter's Field, old man."

"Or Forest Lawn, either. I don't want to be buried with trash."

"You want to know in front?"

"Punk! What do you think I am?"

"I'm sorry . . . I'm sorry, old man. I know what you are. You're the most man I ever knew."

"That's okay, Wes. I know why you said that. The same thing as pulling me out of that room, huh? It's no good anymore, son."

As if by mutual consent, they walked toward the corner of the garage farthest from the street. The old man calmly seated himself in his beloved old leather chair, lit a twisted black cigar, and inhaled deeply. He moved his lips, trying to smile up at Wesley.

Wesley screwed the silencer into the .45 and cocked the piece. He held it dead-level pointed at Pet's forehead.

"Goodbye, Pop. Say hello to Carmine for me."

"I will, son. Don't stay out too late."

The slug slammed above the bridge of the old man's nose, precisely at the point where his dark eyebrows just failed to meet. The impact rocked the chair against the wall, and the old man slumped to the floor. Wesley picked him up in his arms. He was carrying the old man's body toward the door to the first floor when he noticed the deep trench cut into the concrete. He laid the old man on his back in the trench and pressed the still-warm pistol into his hand.

Wesley shoveled the earth back into the trench until it was ten inches from the top. Then he began to mix the new batch of concrete.

It was all finished inside of an hour, the floor now smoothed and drying in the heat of the 3400K spot-lights attached to the back beams.

Wesley went over and sat in the old man's chair. He watched the concrete harden, fingering Pet's cutoff shotgun.

The kid let himself into the garage the next day, silently and quickly, as he had been taught. For the first time in his memory, the old man wasn't there. He heard the slightest of sounds and whirled in the opposite direc-tion, hitting the floor, his pistol up and ready. He saw nothing.

"Too slow, kid."

"Wesley?" the kid questioned, as the other man emerged from the shadows, now dressed in the outfit he last wore on the roof.

"Yeah. Put the piece down."

"Where's Pet?"

"Gone home."

"Like he wanted to in the . . . ?"

"You knew, huh? Good. Yeah, like that. Now it's just me."

"And me, right?"

"If you want."

"What else could I . . . ?"

"It's different now, kid. We got all of them, but there's still something else to work on. You know what?"

"I figure I'll learn that from you."

"Where's your father?"

"My father's been dead for twenty years. At least that's what they said."

"Your mother?"

"She went after him."

"Who raised you?"

"The State."

"Okay. From now on, you live here. You handle the cars. Pet taught you, right?"

"Last time I was here, he said he'd taught me all he knew . . . and that you'd teach me the rest."

"The rest of what *I* know. And then you . . ."

"I know."

"From now on, I'm the outside-man, right? You're gone—nobody sees you, got it?"

"Yes."

"You got your stuff?"

"All my weapons are here already, except my carry-piece. All my clothes, too."

Wesley led the kid to the now indistinguishable spot on the floor under which the old man lay buried.

"The old man's there," he said, pointing.

"Seems like he should have—"

"What? A fucking headstone? A monument? He left his monument on Chrystie Street."

"I know."

"Then *act* like you know," Wesley told him, unconsciously imitating the old man.

The kid turned away without another word. "Who fucked up the Ford? It's too shiny for—"

"Fix it. Fix all of them. You know what to do."

"You going to do what Pet did?"

"I can't. I can't talk to people like that. But for right now I don't have to. You know all the systems?"

"Pet showed me last week."

Wesley faded from the garage, leaving the kid alone.

That same night, Wesley wheeled the back-to-matte Ford down Water Street and took the FDR toward the Brooklyn Bridge. He met the man with the money from the Mansfield job in front of City Hall, on lower Broadway. The man climbed into the back seat of the Ford and handed twenty-five thousand across to Wesley as the car pulled away.

"You want another job?" the man asked.

"Who, how much time I got, and how much?"

"You hit kids?"

"Same three questions," Wesley said, flat-voiced. "Answer them or split."

"It's not actually a hit—it's a snatch. You got to—"

"No good."

"No good? You haven't even *heard*—"

"Get out," Wesley told the man as he pulled over to the curb.

"Hey! Fuck you, man. I'm not getting out, and you're

not blasting me in the middle of the fucking city, either. Now, just—"

Wesley pulled a cable under the dash and the back seat of the four-door sedan whipped forward on its greased rails, propelled by twelve five-hundred-pound test-steel springs. The front seat was triple-bolted to reinforced steel beams in the floor—it weighed six hundred pounds.

The effect was like being thrown into a solid steel wall at forty miles per hour.

The man's entire chest cavity was crushed like an eggshell. Wesley turned and shoved the seat backward with both hands; with the steel springs released from their tension, it clicked back into place. The dead man remained plastered against the plastic slipcover of the front seat. Another quick shove and he was on the floor. Wesley tugged at a pull cord, and the body was covered with a black canvas tarp. The whole operation took well under a minute.

Wesley had never turned off the engine. He put the car in gear and moved off. His first thought was simply to drive the car into the garage as it was and let the kid handle the disposal. But then he remembered that the kid had to be protected, as Wesley himself had been protected.

He deliberately drove the Ford under the shadows of the Manhattan Bridge. It looked like a prowl car "undercovers" would drive—there was some immediate rustling in the shadows when he pulled in. *Too* much rustling.

Wesley pulled out again and hit the Drive. He rolled along until he came to the Avenue D Projects, took the off-ramp, and turned back the way he'd come. Back at the Projects, he pointed the car down the private path that only the Housing Authority cops were supposed to use. No one challenged the car.

Wesley drove until he saw an unoccupied bench. He stopped the car and got out. After a quick scan, he pulled the dead man out and propped him up convincingly on the bench. The man's head fell down on his crushed chest—not an unfamiliar sight after dark.

Wesley drove out of the Projects without trouble and was back inside the garage in minutes. The kid came out of the shadows with his grease gun; he lowered the barrel when he saw the Ford.

"Don't ever drop your guard unless you see it's me, understand? Don't be looking at any fucking *car*!"

The kid said nothing.

"It might've been seen," Wesley told him. "I had to use the springs. It's got to be painted with new plates and maybe some—"

"I know what to do," the kid interrupted, on surer ground now.

Wesley went back to his own place.

It wasn't hard to find humans who wanted problems disposed of and expected to pay for the service, but the process was hard on Wesley. All the bargaining—they *always* tried that—the jabber-jabber, the need they all had to "explain."

It wasn't like before, when Pet had fronted it off. Wesley tried the Times Square bars first, but he couldn't mesh, even with the freaks. The way they looked at him, the way they moved aside when they saw him coming—it told him his face was still too flat and his eyes still too cold.

The stubby blonde hustler was working her way down the end of the long bar, her flesh-padded hips gently bumping anyone who looked remotely like he'd go for a minimal financial investment. When she got to Wesley, he turned and tried a smile.

"Sit down," he told her. "Have a drink."

"Aw . . . Look, baby, I got to go to the little girls' room. Order me a Pink Lady and I'll be right back."

Less than ten minutes later, the truth came to Wesley. He went back out into the night.

Inside the warehouse, Wesley methodically went through all the papers the old man had left. He found a fine-ruled notebook with a black plastic cover. The first page said "CLIENTS," and each succeeding page was devoted to a single individual: name, addresses, phone numbers—business and home—and other miscellaneous information. He also saw prices next to each name:

LEWISTON, PETER . . . $25K+
RANDOLPH, MARGARET . . . $40K

It took Wesley a long time to go through the book, figuring which people he had already worked for—he had never known names except when it was absolutely necessary to the job. Slowly and carefully, he extracted enough data to put together a list of the jobs they had never done. Had Pet kept a list of potentials?

The only area codes Wesley saw next to the phone numbers were 516, 914, 201, and 203. Long Island, Westchester, northern New Jersey, southern Connecticut. The seven-digit numbers Wesley assumed were 212—anywhere within the five boroughs.

The next night, Wesley prepared to try all the 516 numbers. He didn't take the Ford—it was *too* nondescript. And the Eldorado was a little too hard to miss. He couldn't drive the cab like Pet, make it seem as if he belonged behind the wheel, although the kid could.

Finally, he settled on the Firebird—a chocolate-brown 1970 model with a worked-over undercarriage and very sticky radial tires. He checked the electromagnets, releasing the pistol they held in place, then returned it under the dash. He put six rolls of dimes and five rolls of quarters in the glove compartment and stashed a long, rectangular gray metal box full of equipment in the console between the seats.

Wesley took the Brooklyn Bridge to the BQE, connecting to the Long Island Expressway. He was wearing a dark blue J. Press summer-weight suit with a light-blue knit shirt, no tie. It all fit well with the car, as did the complete set of credit cards that matched his comeback-clean driver's license and registration.

"You can't fucking beat that American Express Gold for impressing the rollers, Wes. Any sucker can cop the

Green, but the Gold is for high-class faggots. The Man sees that, he figures you not the right guy to roust." If Wesley was surprised that Pet's words ran through his mind the way Carmine's did, it didn't show on his face.

He kept the car just past the speed limit all the way to Exit 40. From there it was only a mile or so to the giant Gertz parking lot. He picked out one of the outdoor phone booths near the back. The area was empty except for a gang of kids listening to their car radios, all tuned to the same station. It was loud, but it wouldn't disturb conversation inside the booth.

Wesley quickly swept the booth with the tiny scanner Pet had shown him how to use—it was clean. A hard twist removed the mouthpiece; then Wesley inserted the flat metal disc with its network of printed circuits and perforations which exactly matched the original. Voiceprints were getting to be as much of a problem as fingerprints, and staying ahead was the same as staying alive.

The first number was a busy signal; the second, no answer. The third was in Hewlett Harbor. A soft-voiced woman picked up the phone.

"Hello."

"Could I speak with Mr. Norden, please?" Wesley asked, just politely enough.

"May I tell him who is calling?"

"Mr. Petraglia."

The phone was silent for almost thirty seconds; Wesley was going to give it forty-five and then hang up. A clipped, hard voice came on the line: "Do you think it was wise to give your name like that?"

"Would you have come to the phone otherwise?" Wesley replied.

"You're not . . ."

"I'm his brother. In the same business. He told me to call you."

"Well, I still have the problem, but time is getting . . ."

"This is all the talking I do on the phone. Tell me where to meet you."

"Can you be at the Sequoia Club in an hour? You know where it is?"

"In one hour."

"Listen! How will I know you? Do you—?"

"Just go in the back and sit down," Wesley told him. "I'll find you."

"Look, I—"

Wesley replaced the receiver, first exchanging the voice-alteration disc with the stock item. The shiny chrome of the phone coin box picked up fingerprints perfectly. Wesley knew smearing them was better than wiping them—a pristine surface would be a message all its own. A man wearing gloves in the summer making a phone call would be too much for even a Nassau County cop to pass up. But you could see their orange-and-blue squad cars coming a hundred yards away.

Pet's book had all the information about the Sequoia, and Wesley had thoroughly checked it out on a street map of Norden's area before driving out to the Island. He dialed his mind to dismiss all the information he had

memorized on the first two people he had called, focusing on what he knew about Norden.

There wasn't much, except the price was the highest
in the 516 section: "$100K." And a code: "P/ok," which
Wesley took to mean that Norden had used this service
previously and had paid off without incident.

As Wesley approached the Firebird, he took in the
three kids sitting on its hood and fenders. When he got
closer, he looked into their faces and got blank, vicious
smiles in return—they were bullies, not predators, still
too young to see what the Times Square hustler had
instantly recognized. They nudged each other as Wesley came even closer, sliding off the Firebird at the last
moment.

They were smiling when Wesley took out the keys
and opened the door. They kept smiling as he started
the engine. And never noticed that Wesley hadn't fully
closed the door—his left foot was pressing out against
it with nearly all his strength, held in check only by the
slightly greater pressure of his left hand and forearm
locked onto the door handle from the inside.

The three kids assembled in front of the driver's door.
Still smiling, their leader motioned for Wesley to lower
the window. Wesley flicked the power-window switch on
the center console with his right hand, and the tinted
glass whispered down. The leader came up to the window, flanked by his partners.

"Say, mister, could you help us out?" he sneered.
"We need a hundred bucks for a cup of coffee." The

other two laughed nervously, their hands in their jacket pockets.

Wesley looked up; the veins in his forearm were popping full under the suit coat's jacket. "Get the fuck outta here, punk," he said softly.

The leader whipped out a switchblade in what he thought was a lightning move. It was so unprofessionally slow and so stupidly flashy that Wesley had to make himself wait—he didn't want to fire any shots in the parking lot. The kid was about two feet from the door when Wesley suddenly released his left hand. One hundred and fifty pounds of reinforced steel swinging on siliconed ball bearings smashed the kid from his knees to his waist, throwing him back against his partners. Wesley flicked the selector lever into gear and the Firebird screamed off, fishtailing slightly to get traction. He was up to fifty in seconds, leaving the two kids bending over their fallen partner.

Wesley turned left out of the parking lot, heading for the North Shore. More trouble to kill them than not to. They weren't about to go to the police, not those kind. They'd lick their wounds, contenting themselves with their punk visions of hot revenge that would never happen. Wesley's mind flashed back to the clerk in the Roxy Hotel. He banished the thought, concentrating.

The uniformed parking-lot attendant gave him a "Thank you, sir!" and a stamped ticket in exchange for his car key. Surrendering the key didn't make Wesley uncomfortable—he had a duplicate in his coat pocket.

Pet's book said this wasn't a membership club. Sure enough, Wesley slid through the huge front door without incident. Inside, it was like any other bar. It may have been way upscale, Wesley thought, but there must be places to fade into, just like there were in the Hudson River waterfront joints he had grown up in. The J. Press suit would hold him unless someone tried to strike up a conversation. The part-of-the-package Rolex told him that Norden should have already been there for thirteen minutes, so he went into the large, dimly lit room with the horseshoe-shaped bar looking for a man sitting alone.

There weren't many. The brunette hostess swayed over to the space Wesley was occupying. She looked like a high-class version of the Times Square hustler, and Wesley tried hard not to catch her eye. She tried just as hard to catch his . . . and succeeded. Her smile was bright and professional, and her appraisal of his clothing was so quick as to seem instinctive. Pet had told him that the best knife-men were a combination of breeding and practice—he guessed her skill was acquired the same way. She took his order, brought his rye and ginger to him quickly: "Would you like this mixed, sir?"

"No, thanks."

Wesley didn't pick up any fear reaction from her at all. He suddenly realized that he must be as foreign to these people as a man from Venus. They weren't looking for a shark in their swimming pool, so they didn't see one. Wesley relaxed and smiled, and the hostess flashed him a genuine-looking smile in return. *That must take a lot of practice,* he thought admiringly. He watched her as she glided away, her hips gently swaying, not wiggling the way Wesley had expected. *Very good,* he thought, wondering where she'd learned.

Wesley had the Norden candidates narrowed down to a field of three, but Pet's written description could have fit any of them. They all looked alike to Wesley anyway. He was about to find a pay phone when he noticed the hostess bringing a phone with a short cord to another patron at the far end of the bar. She smiled and plugged it in somewhere behind the bar. The man immediately picked up the receiver and started talking.

Wesley had left the change from a twenty on the bar. He didn't want the liquor, but he needed to get the hostess's attention. So he threw back the rye, hardening his throat—it slipped down so smoothly he felt it must have been watered.

The hostess caught his eye before he could raise his hand or his voice. She was in front of him in a flash.

"Could you refill this?" Wesley asked her. "And get me a phone, please?"

"Certainly, sir."

She was back with both, reduced Wesley's seventeen dollars down to fourteen, and was gone again, leaving another smile trailing behind before Wesley could even crank up his face to respond.

He noted that there was no number on the phone's dial. Wesley dialed the Sequoia Club direct, and told the professionally nice voice that answered that he would like to have Mr. Norden paged.

"It'll be just a moment, sir," the voice told him, and then he heard the mechanism telling him he was on hold. Wesley signaled the hostess. She signaled back "just a minute," and went out from behind the bar to carry a phone over to a beefy-looking man sitting at a small round table alone in the back.

She bent over farther than seemed absolutely necessary to plug in the instrument, but the man was too distracted to notice. Wesley watched him pick up the receiver, then he heard "Yes?" in his ear.

"I'll be there in a minute," Wesley responded.

"Who is this?"

Wesley hung up. He saw Norden speaking into a dead phone for a couple of seconds, then watched as the man gently replaced the receiver. Wesley walked over to Norden's table. He could get no real sense of the depth of the room, and he had to decide between watching the wall behind them or the entrance. He took the second choice and sat down.

Norden looked intently at Wesley: "You're . . . ?"

"The man on the telephone," Wesley answered.

"How do I know who you really are?"

"Mr. P. gave me your name and number, that should be enough. And it's all you're going to get."

"Okay, okay. Look, I don't want to talk in here."

"The parking lot?"

"I'll meet you out there in five minutes."

"Forget that. We walk out together, or you won't see me again."

"You don't think I'd . . ."

Wesley didn't answer. He kept both hands flat on top of the little round table, a gesture as incomprehensible to Norden as Wesley's earlier threat had been. Norden signaled to the hostess, who immediately came over. She gave Wesley an extra-bright smile and took the twenty Norden handed her. She didn't pretend she was going to make change. Wesley wished he was negotiating with her instead of this weasel.

They hit the outside door, copping a "Goodnight, sir!" to each of them from several different flunkies, and then they were in the lot. When the attendant left with their tickets and Norden's five-dollar bill, Wesley couldn't tell if this was meant to cover both of them, so he paid nothing.

"Drive up the road about a half-mile and pull over," he told Norden. "I'll be right behind you and we'll talk."

Norden started to answer, then apparently thought better of it. His white Cadillac Coupe de Ville was easy to follow; Wesley counted six-tenths of a mile on his odometer before the Caddy pulled off to the side. It was a wide field that Wesley thought was a farm until he spotted the stone gate, set in about fifty yards from the road.

Wesley pulled the Firebird just in front of Norden's car, then backed up so that the Caddy couldn't leave first without reversing.

"Pull up your hood so it looks like I'm helping you with the engine. In case somebody stops," Wesley told him, opening his own trunk.

"Who would stop?"

"The cops, right?"

"Not around here, they wouldn't. Anyway, that's not important. It's my wife, she—" Wesley started to say it didn't matter, but some almost dormant instinct told him that this rich man needed to talk or there'd be no contract—"she has all the money, really. It used to be all right, but now she's getting older and crazier and I can't . . . look, will you do it?"

"Yes."

"Can you make it look like an accident?"

"No. I'm no mechanic—you're going to be someplace else at the time. It'll look like a robbery or"—watching Norden's face—"a rape that went wrong. . . . Something."

"It won't be painful? I wouldn't want—"

"She won't feel a thing. For a hundred thousand dollars."

"That's ridiculous!"

"That's what it costs for a perfect job. She goes, and I say nothing if I'm caught . . . ever."

"Oh, I know the code. Mr. Petraglia told me how you all—"

"Then you know how things work," Wesley cut him off. "Good. I need half up front, in cash. You know what to do: nothing bigger than fifties, no serial numbers in sequence, no new bills. And don't fuck with powders or anything; we got the same lights as the feds."

"I wouldn't do anything like that. . . . But it'll be hard to raise that kind of cash without making her suspicious."

The woman was no longer "my wife," Wesley noticed. "So what? She won't be around long enough to do anything about it."

"I need a week. Can I meet you right here next Tuesday night?"

"No. I'll wait a week. Stay by your phone; I'll call between nine and nine-thirty one night, tell you where to come."

"But . . . I guess that's the way you—"

Wesley cut him off by walking away. He closed the Firebird's trunk and drove off. On the way back, he thought the whole thing over. Maybe Norden's car was wired; maybe they were picking up his conversation with a shotgun mike from behind that stone fence; maybe . . .

But they'd never play even *that* square with him. Wesley knew he'd never die in prison, because he'd never come to trial. He thought about the mark's "code" and wondered where Pet had gotten the stones to shovel that much crap. He remembered Carmine telling him about the "code."

"What fucking 'code,' kid? Here in prison? Shit! The 'code' that says skinners can't walk the Yard? You know DeMayo? That miserable slime fucked a four-year-old girl until she died from being ripped open. He walks the Yard and nobody says nothing. Why? Because he carries and he kills. That much for the fucking 'code'! You know why cons always target baby-rapers? Because they're usually such sorry bastards—old, sick, weak, with no crew Outside. Or young and fucked up in the brain, you know? The kind that can't protect themselves. And this bullshit that the cons fuck them up because they love kids, or 'cause they 'got kids of their own'? Crap! They kill them and they rip them off because they are fucking

*weak. . . . That's the only rule in here. There's no 'code.'
There's no fucking nothing . . . except this"*—a tightly
balled fist—*"this"*—a flat-edged hand—*"this"*—the first
two fingers rubbed against the thumb in the universal
symbol for money. *"And you handle it all with this!"*—
tapping his temple.

"What about this?" Wesley had asked, smacking his
fist against his chest.

"Kid, all the heart does is pump blood," Carmine told
him. "Listen, take this racial shit, all right? A nigger
can't walk certain places, right? So how come Lee, he
walks where he wants?"

"I don't know."

"Because he won't be fucked with, that's why. He
don't mind dying. That's the only thing they respect,
kid . . . in here and out there."

"You said a few things with your hands."

"They're all the same thing: power. You got it and
you don't use it, it goes away. You *do* use it, it grows.
And if you don't have it, you better get some."

"Who do you get it from?"

"Power in America is money. You can steal money,
all the money in the world, but you'll never be able to
join their fucking rich-man's club. You could steal a bil-
lion fucking dollars and not run for office . . . but you
can *buy* a senator, you see?"

"So what kind of power could I get? My freedom?"

"Not freedom, Wes, free*doom*. People like us are never
free to say how we live; but some of us can say how we
die. And when. That's the only thing really free for us.

Out there, or in here. And those are the only two places in the world—out there or in here."

"Is the whole 'code' really fucked up that bad? When I was in the reform school, we—"

"It's *all* gone now. Look around the Yard, what do you see? Me, I see maggots—garbage that would sell your life for a carton, never mind a parole. I see junkies, walking around dead. I see colored guys in here for *being* colored, and little kids in here for bullshit beefs, just because they had no coin. The only real criminals are Outside anyway. Things have changed. You don't see the man who steals anymore, the good clean thief, the professional. No, it's all ragged out, Wes. It's all gone sick, and it's not gonna ever get better."

Wesley realized that Norden didn't know any of this—to a mark, the movie mythology was gospel truth.

When Wesley pressed the horn ring and slid inside the garage, the kid was waiting for him. He had the grease gun leveled—it didn't flicker until Wesley stepped out into the soft glow of the diffused spots.

"Okay?" the kid asked.

"Only thing may be a make on the plates and the car color. We can't use those plates again, but otherwise . . ."

"I'll take care of it."

It took Wesley only fifteen minutes to reach his own place, shower, dispose of the clothing, snap a leash on the dog, and return to the garage. He led the dog to a spot right in front of the garage door, unsnapped the leash, said "Watch!"

"You got the right kind of clothes for the roof?" he asked the kid.

"This time of night?"

Wesley nodded.

"Yeah. In the chest of drawers over there."

"Get dressed and meet me up there, okay?"

The kid walked over to the chest, still carrying the grease gun in one hand.

"I'm going to meet a guy from Pet's old client book," Wesley told the kid. "About a week from tonight. He wants me to hit his wife. I told him fifty K up front. I'll call and tell him where to bring it. I figure he'll be looking for the same car. You follow me with the Caddy. I'll have him meet me in a field somewhere out there. You bring the nightscope and a quiet rifle. Anything happens, you hit him and split . . . okay?"

"Why we going to hit his wife?"

"For the money."

"There's a risk, right?"

"Always a risk."

"So why risk? I could just as easy pop him soon as he gets out of his car. Then we got fifty thousand and no risk."

"That's good thinking, kid. There's no code, we don't owe the sucker nothing. But if he's bought himself some cover and you hit him, we're in a firefight. And that's a *bigger* risk, right?"

"Yeah," the kid said. "I see."

"So what we do is take the weasel's money and just don't make the hit. We just disappear."

"And we get the fifty thousand."

"Yeah."

"Somehow it don't seem right."

"Not to hit the wife?"

"Not to hit *him*. It don't seem safe to leave him around."

"Don't think like a sucker. This is no hit on a mob guy. What's he gonna do, fucking *sue* us? He wouldn't *begin* to know where to look for me. A trail of bodies is easier to follow than a trail of rumors."

"But he's seen your face."

"Kid, he never saw my face."

After the kid went back downstairs, Wesley stayed on the roof to focus on the choices he had.

If he took the money from Norden and just walked away without fulfilling the contract, the overwhelming odds were that Norden would never be in a position to retaliate. He would never see Wesley again, or even hear of him.

But Pet's established business had been based upon two foundations: regular employment by the conservative old men who formed an ever-loosening and sloppy fraternity, and occasional jobs from an even sloppier and far hungrier group of wealthy humans . . . his client list.

Maybe that group depended on their own telegraph for information? Wesley's failure to carry out a contract might curtail future employment.

It wasn't nearly as simple as he had represented it to the kid. But the kid had to be taught to think a few steps in advance, and this was the best way to teach him. Wesley calculated the cash he and Pet had hidden in various spots throughout the building, in stashes elsewhere in the city, and in various banks and safe-deposit boxes around the country. Wesley could put his hands on almost half a million and never leave the building, but he could hardly bank the whole thing and expect to live on the interest. Even this huge sum of money was nothing compared with what they had actually earned in their profession. Pet routinely discounted all payoffs from employers against the possibility that the money was somehow marked, in serial sequence, or just plain bogus.

The discounters charged 70 percent for brand-new money with sequential serial numbers, all the way down to 20 percent for money that looked, felt, and smelled used. They, in turn, deposited the money with a number of foreign banks—banks of friendly South American governments ran a close second to those in the Caribbean. Pet had laughed out loud once, before reading Wesley a *Times* article about the "unstable" governments in South America:

"Simple-ass *educated* motherfuckers! Listen to this, Wes. The fools talk about *predicting* which countries is stable and which ain't. Now any asshole could tell you that if he would just ask the discounters. Wherever *they* put their money, you know there ain't going to be no fucking revolution."

"I thought you said some of them banked in Haiti."

"So?"

"So how about if that Papa Du takes it all and tells them to go fuck themselves?"

"No way. Why you think America sends troops in there like they do? So many rich motherfuckers got their money in that place, and it's those same rich bastards who bankroll the politicians. They're all criminals."

"Like us."

"Wrong. Stealing to eat ain't criminal—stealing to be rich is."

"I wanted to get rich."

"So's you wouldn't have to . . . ?"

"Steal. Yeah, okay, old man."

The money they got in exchange was perfect: old, used, no way to distinguish it or connect it with any job or payoff. "Steam-cleaned," they called it. Such money always came with a lifetime guarantee—the lifetime of the laundryman.

So the half-million was clean. They could pass it all day, anyplace, without trouble. Pet had made some watertight containers for the cash, and Wesley had memorized the locations. And the bank accounts and safe-deposit boxes all had books, keys, and papers to grease the way if necessary. So they didn't have to kill to eat, to survive, even to live in what would amount to a certain degree of luxury and comfort.

Wesley often thought about foreign countries, but

never with longing. The only piece of land he would risk his life to protect was an ugly old warehouse on Pike Slip.

So why kill Norden . . . why meet him at all? What could another fifty thousand—forty at best, after the cleaning—what could that mean to either of them now?

But Carmine had built a bomb in hell—a bomb that had somehow learned how to explode and kill without destroying itself. Wesley sat on the roof, thinking: *Is that the only fucking thing I can do now?*

Carmine had spent hours examining, probing, destroying Wesley's once-treasured genetic misconceptions: *"The only color I hate is blue."* And Wesley spent still more hours wrestling with them on his own. What made Carmine hate the men who had perished in their custom-made gas chamber was easy to see. They had left him to die without a cause, without a culture—so the old man forged his own, joining his hatred with Wesley's need.

But what had made the men that Carmine hated? They weren't born like that.

The only common thread in all the humans Wesley had been paid to kill had been their wealth or their threat to those who had wealth. That same thread ran through all the humans Wesley killed intentionally for himself and Carmine and Pet—but it wasn't in every one of the victims. The woman on Sutton Place had died because she was a way to kill others—that she was rich was incidental. The Prince must have had some *serious* money stashed someplace, but he was killed because he was an enemy. The people in the crowd on West 51st who got bombed by the grenade, the junkies blown up by the booby-trapped bag, whoever was within the fall-out range of the building on Chrystie, the methadone clinic, the girl in the massage parlor . . .

Casualties of war. *Very* fucking casual.

When the jets strafed a village in Korea, they left everybody there on the ground, burning. Women breed children; children grow up to hunt their parents' killers. Blood into the ground, seeding the next wave.

They hit a village way up north once, before Wesley got on the sniper team. When his squad charged the smoking ruins, Wesley was on the point. The lieutenant wasn't shit, a ROTC college kid the whole platoon hated, so Wesley just up and took the point because he wanted to stay alive. The silent backing of the rest was enough to educate even a human with a college degree on that miserable slice of earth.

Wesley crashed through first, but the place was empty. In the next-to-last hut, he heard a baby's cry and he hit the ground elbows first, rifle up and pointed at Oriental-chest level. No more sound. Wesley crawled toward the hut . . . slowly.

He saw the woman then; she was coming at him with a tiny knife, moving as quickly and quietly as she could. As Wesley rose to his knees, she launched herself at his face. Wesley spun his rifle and slammed it against the side of her head. She went down hard. He ran past her and started toward the next hut. The woman landed on his back, and her knife pricked into his upper shoulder. He rolled with the thrust; the woman went flying over his back, still holding the knife.

Wesley held the rifle at his waist. His eyes met the woman's . . . and time stopped. He motioned with the barrel for her to split—get into the fucking jungle before he blew her head off. It took her only a second to understand what he meant. The woman moved off, holding the puny knife between herself and Wesley, as though it were a cross to a vampire. But instead of running into the jungle, she backed toward the hut.

Wesley's ears picked up the sound of other soldiers systematically working their way through the burning ruins: shots fired, an occasional scream.

The woman kept backing toward the hut. *Stupid bitch*, he thought. She was going to die or worse if she didn't get into the brush fast. The woman ducked into the hut and came out a second later, holding a naked little male child under her left arm. Her right hand still held the knife. Wesley watched as she faded into the jungle. He was still staring at the spot when the others came up behind him.

On the way back, Wesley forced himself to think about what had happened. He finally realized that the only reason he didn't blow her away at first was because it wasn't consistent with his image of himself to kill a woman. Besides, it was some faraway commander that had talked about wiping them all out. And *he* never went out with the grunts, so fuck him and his orders— *that* was consistent.

But when Wesley saw her face, he had been afraid for just a split second. It wasn't until she came out of the hut that Wesley realized the crazy woman was willing to die to protect the little kid. He remembered her face and her look. If his mother had looked like that, maybe he wouldn't have been raised by the State. But he had never seen his mother as far as he could recall, so he just didn't know. . . .

When they kill only the male children, they make one huge motherfucker of a mistake, he thought.

The next morning, Wesley told the kid they weren't even going to meet Norden, much less cancel his ticket or his wife's. He watched the kid's face closely, pleased to see no trace of disappointment . . . or happiness. It was always bad news when the bomb started to need the target. Then he's just another junkie, needing a different kind of fix—no good to any professional.

But the kid was still puzzled. "So what's the next thing?"

"I don't know, kid. There's a reason why I didn't want to go out with Pet. The methadone clinic was part of it, maybe. And some other stuff, too. It started to come to me just before that hit at the racetrack."

"What stuff?"

"That sicko, the freak who went around here cutting little kids with a razor—you know who I mean?"

"Yeah. They never caught him, right? He's still out there?"

"He's in the morgue. I hit him on the Slip the night I brought the dog home, a long time before you came."

"That was the right thing to do. If I was the fucking heat and I came on him, I'd never bring him in."

"They wouldn't bring *me* in, either, right? And I didn't

hit him for that. *All* dead meat brings flies. To me, he was no different than that methadone clinic."

"Because?"

"Because what I just told you. Baby-rapers bring the Law—at least the ones with money always do. So he had to go. I thought he was cutting on a kid out there. But after I hit him, it turned out to be the dog."

"How'd you know where to look for him?"

"I learned in prison. If I was a cop, there'd be a whole lot of sorry motherfuckers out there."

"How'd you hit him?"

"With the target pistol, at about fifty feet."

"That don't seem right to me. Like you showing him too much respect, you know? You maybe should of slashed his fucking throat."

"He's just as dead this way. You think they'd pin a fucking medal on me for taking him out?"

"No, I know they don't do that."

"They *used* to do it, right? I got a couple of medals in Korea for shit like that . . . stupid."

"For giving you the medals?"

"Me, for doing their fucking killing for them."

"You did Carmine's killing for him. . . ."

"Carmine made it *my* killing, too. And even if it wasn't, I had to kill them, so I could start doing my own."

"At the racetrack?"

"No. I *thought* that was it. But, if it was, I'd go on this Norden thing, right? In fact, that's the one thing been on my mind for a long time."

"Why just that?" the kid asked.

"Meaning . . . ?"

"Why just killing—there's other things."

"That's all I know how to . . . Look, you got a woman?"

"No, not right now. I mean, there's a girl I go and see sometimes, but I can't make anything regular out of it. . . ."

"But you can have one if you want, right? You can talk to them? Talk to all kinds of people out there"—he gestured with a wide sweep of his hand to encompass the city—"right?"

"Just some kind of people, really . . ."

"What kind?"

"Guys that have been Inside, women on the track . . . But . . . I don't know, maybe you're right. I could talk to anybody I wanted, probably."

"I can't."

"Can't what?"

"Have a woman, talk to a man outside the life, be around people and not have them know about me . . . I did it when I went out to see Norden, but that's not because I fit in. To those people, I was just invisible. In Times Square, they all knew.

"And when they don't. . . . You believe that three punks tried to take me off in a parking lot on the Island?"

"Heeled?"

"No!" Wesley snorted. "Three punks and one little knife between them . . . and I'm *already* sitting in the car with the engine running."

"Jesus! They must've been . . ."

"They just couldn't see, kid," Wesley explained. "I could walk right up to them and they'd never know. But I couldn't *talk* to them."

"The women, maybe you could . . ."

"No. I left that. I left it in prison, or maybe even before."

"You could get it back."

"It would cost too much now. And what would I do with it? I know what I have to do, kid. Just not *who* to do it to."

"I don't know, either," the kid said.

"Well, you better fucking find out. Carmine sent me to the library to find out *how* to do some things. I guess you'd better start going to find out *who*."

"I haven't had a woman since I moved in here."

"You better stay in touch with that, too, kid. Stay in touch; stay close to it all. After I go, you don't want to be all alone."

"Wesley . . . ?"

"Carmine and Pet were always together, right? I was alone until I had them. When Carmine checked out, he left Pet behind. And Pet left me behind for you, understand? When I go, you'll be alone. We don't have enough bullets for them all, kid. It was all for fucking nothing unless you can make it happen—I know that now. I had to avenge Carmine. I did that. So how come I'm not dead? Home with him?"

"I don't know, but . . ."

"Pet wouldn't have gone unless he knew that I was okay to keep on. I can't go, either, not until you are."

"I'm not ready—you've still got stuff to show me."

"Show you what? I've taught you just about everything I know about how to kill."

"But . . ."

"But there has to be something more, right?"

"Yeah."

"Well, that's the mystery, kid. The part I don't know about. But I'm going to figure it out before I leave."

"Politics?" the kid asked.

"Politics? I don't know. I know this: When I was overseas, I learned some things besides killing. Say it takes thirty grains of rice a day to keep a man alive . . . what happens if you give him forty grains?"

"He's happy?"

"Enough not to kill you, anyway. What happens if you give him twenty grains?"

"Then he comes for you."

"Okay, sure. But why the fuck should he spare your life for thirty lousy grains of rice? Why shouldn't he want the whole thing for himself and grow his *own* damn rice?"

"People own land. . . ."

"Is that right? And where'd they get it from?"

"Bought it? Or it got left to them?"

"From who? You keep going back far enough, kid, what you find out is, somebody fought for it."

"So?"

"So why don't the sorry motherfuckers getting the thirty grains of rice fight for it, too?"

"The law—"

"The law was written by the people who got the land *now*, see?"

"Yeah. And they got the police and the Army and everything else to protect that land."

"That isn't all, kid. What d'you think the Welfare

Department is all about? Or the fucking methadone. Any of that giveaway shit?"

"I don't see how it's the same. If—"

"The Welfare, that's the thirty grains of rice. You can live *off* it but you can't live *on* it, you understand? And the methadone, to a dope fiend, *that's* the thirty grains."

"Dope fiends don't vote, Wes."

"The fuck they don't. Winos vote on Election Day, right?"

"Yeah, for a bottle of wine."

"So the dope fiends . . ."

"I get it."

"Yeah. So what? Even *I* can see that."

"What do you mean, Wesley?"

"That kind of crap just plain hits you in the face. They got to have *systems*, you know? Like in the joint. Just a few hacks to cover a fucking regiment of cons, right? But nobody ever walks over the Wall."

"The guards have the guns."

"Bullshit! They don't have the guns in the blocks, not on the tiers. Those guards are unarmed, but we let them do whatever they do, because we don't even trust each other. It's real easy my way—black and white, us against them, period.

"I did it for Carmine . . . but now I don't know who to do it for. It can't be for me. . . ."

"Why not? If you risk your life like you do, then . . ."

"I'm already dead. I'm tired. I don't want to be here anymore, kid."

"I don't understand that."

"I know. That means you can still be here, you see? It can still be for you."

Wesley went upstairs and focused on the fourth-floor wall for a long while. Then he went down to the kid's room in the garage.

"I saw on the news last night that Papa Du's faggot son is coming to this country."

"From Haiti?" the kid asked.

"Yeah. That fat, greasy nigger is running the show down there his way. I knew a guy in the joint that lived under his old man—he said this Papa Du was the Devil, straight up."

"So?"

"I'm going to blow up his kid."

"Why? I don't get it, Wesley. You call him a nigger, right? And all that's going to be getting anything behind you wasting this cocksucker is *another* bunch of niggers. . . ."

"Like Carmine said to me once. That maggot, he *is* a nigger. An ugly word for a black bastard with a greedy heart and bloody hands. But the others he's got locked up there, they ain't niggers, kid—they're people like us, right? Like you, anyway."

"You going to hit him for . . . ?"

"I wish it was for me. Maybe it will be for me after it happens. If it works in Haiti . . ."

"Hit the Boss here?"

"You know, it's not that hard. I studied assassinations for years. Every day, every way. The reason we don't hit presidents here too often is that we're afraid to die. If the Law doesn't find you, the people who hired you will. The last one, that's just what they did.

"But in some countries, they do it all the time. Look at the different styles. You're going to hit a big man here, how you do it?"

"A sniper rifle," the kid replied. "Like at the bridge."

"Right. But south of the border, you take a goddamn machete and you jump right into the bastard's limo, or up on the stage, or . . ."

"But you'd never—"

"Get out alive?" Wesley interrupted. "But, see, you're not doing it for money. You got some *people* you're protecting—your mother and your children and your neighbors and all that, right? So it's worth it . . . it fucking *must* be worth it."

"It don't seem to work here—that guy who shot Wallace . . ."

"He was a wacko, kid. A stone freak, probably came behind pulling the trigger. He wasn't a pro. I was that close, I'd have so much lead into him it'd take a fucking magnetic crane to get him off the ground."

"That one who shot the black preacher, wasn't he . . . ?"

"That was a fix, kid—just like at some fights, when the odds get long enough. What happened was, somebody came to him in the joint, told him he was pulling The Book anyway, didn't have nothing to lose. So here's the proposition: he hits the preacher and escapes, he's not just ahead, he's rich. He takes the job, and they agree in front not to total him if they make the capture. All he gets is another stretch. You can't do no more than one Life, right? Never see Death Row. And in *that* joint, he's a fucking hero behind hitting that preacher, too.

"Kid, you know how hard it is to hit a man and walk away from it. You know how long I've worked at it. And that's just here. I wouldn't drive no fucking *registered* car to Memphis, hit him with that lousy gun he had, and then try the phony-passport thing. He didn't even have a safe house to crawl into. No cover, nothing. The slob only fired one shot, too. Then he panicked and ran.

"Just a fucking redneck jerk that got used, kid. Just one of the bullets."

"That book I read about it said—"

"A book! Jesus, books are good for science, but they ain't shit for truth. I'll prove it to you. . . . You're always reading about crime, right?"

"Especially about murders . . ."

"Okay. Tell me what you know about the Taylor Twins murder."

"Right. Two rich broads get all ripped up in their fancy apartment. The cops snag this black guy in Brooklyn. He's retarded and scared. They beat a confession outta him, but they can't make it stand up, because there was some real obvious bullshit going on, and he gets cut loose. Anyway, to make it short, they finally get the actual killer, a Puerto Rican junkie. He 'confesses' . . . and he goes down for Double Life upstate."

"Yeah. And here's the truth. Whitmore was the name

of the black guy, right? And Robles was the name of the Latin dude, right?"

"Right. They even had a TV show on about it."

"Okay. Now, understand this—Robles didn't kill those girls."

"How you know that?"

"Because I know the guy who did it. Pet and I did a job for him—it was hitting this old man. See, the old man was all mobbed up, and he found this rich freak had tortured his daughter . . . for fun. Anyway, the girl didn't die, so the outfit wouldn't allow the freak to be killed, just messed up. But the old man wasn't going for that; he put out a contract on his own. But the people found out, and they paid us to hit the old man. They fixed it so's the freak would pay us direct, you understand?"

"Dirty motherfuckers," the kid snarled.

"That's the way they do their business, kid. Anyway, when I went to this apartment—must have had twenty rooms in it—the weasel treated me like I was like *him.* You know, another fucking sex-torture freak? He told me he used to go to their apartment and tie the both of them up—you know, like it was okay with them. At least that's what he said. Anyway, one time he got carried away and wasted them. He even kept some of their things in his place. For trophies, like. He was laughing his ass off at Robles doing time for all that."

"What did you do?"

"I did him."

"For Robles?"

"For me. The freak was really bent out of shape,

and I didn't know what he'd do next. And he'd seen my face. I was going to write to Robles or something, but I got the word that some people wanted him to stay down for that job, and I couldn't do it without exposing myself."

"Jesus."

"Yeah. Jesus. The poor sonofabitch Robles. I heard later he flipped out. They got his ass up in Matteawan."

"Isn't there something . . . ?"

"Maybe. I'm going to hit Fat Boy. Then we'll see."

The next morning found Wesley driving the Caddy up the West Side Highway toward Times Square. Fat Boy was going to arrive in America by boat to promote Haiti's new shipping industry. He was slated to arrive at the Grace Line Pier on the luxury liner *Liberté*. Wesley had planned to get as close to the scene as he could. But as he passed by Pier 40 on the highway, his eye caught a new building apparently under construction right across from the pier.

He turned off the highway at 23rd Street and drove back downtown until he was parked on a narrow street behind the rear of the new building. It was almost finished. In deference to New York tradition, the windows hadn't been put in yet—not much sense doing that without a full-time security guard.

Wesley counted eight stories. A tractor-trailer rumbled by, on its way to one of the waterfront warehouses.

Wesley walked across the street to a steel door set

flush into the back of the building. It was freshly painted red, with a new Yale lock. He opened the door as if he belonged there, and went inside. It was only moderately noisy—the construction crew had just about finished, and only the final touches remained. Wesley had a few quick seconds to notice an unfinished staircase leading to higher floors before a small man with an enormous beer belly screamed over to him, "Hey! You from Collicci's?"

"Yeah!" Wesley shouted back.

"Where's the stuff?"

"In the truck. Be right back."

Wesley was a couple of blocks away before the man inside had time to give things another thought. He drove all the way down to where they were finishing the World Trade Center's Twin Towers, then reversed his field and drove by the front of the building again. It was a long shot to the pier, but not anything all that spectacular.

That night, Wesley made the run again and found the building was completely dark. Fat Boy was due to arrive in two days—that would make it a Saturday. The papers said twelve noon.

The kid was waiting for him when he pulled into the garage. "You still going ahead with it?"

"Yeah. For sure now. It's easy as hell to get in. And there's a clear shot from the top floor, with plenty of room up there . . . perfect. You got the schedule?"

"Yeah," the kid said. "He's supposed to arrive at noon, but it could be as much as an hour and a half later, depending on the ocean. Weather report says fair and clear, high in the eighties, low in the high seventies. The mayor's going to welcome him, and there's going to be a big crowd. And a big demonstration, too."

"Who?" Wesley asked.

"Some exiled Haitians who think this country shouldn't let him come. . . ."

"They'll be glad he did."

"Where'll I be?"

"Right here, watching the TV for the news. Aren't they going to cover it live?"

"Yeah, fuck that! Why should I be here?"

"I don't need you."

"You got the whole thing figured?"

"Yeah, I told you I did. You got the sextant?"

"Look, Wesley, I got *everything* you said. But you left out something."

"What?"

"After you hit him, right? How you going to come out?"

"I guess I'm not."

"No good."

"No good! What the fuck do you mean, 'no good'? Who're you to—?"

"I know who I am. . . . And this is fucked up, Wesley. It's not what you said."

Wesley watched the kid carefully. "How isn't it?"

"You killing this faggot as an *experiment*, right? Sure, it'll maybe help a bunch of other people . . . but you're going to *see*, right? If it works, *then* we're going someplace else, right? That rifle's no machete, Wesley. And you're no Latin American, either."

"Look, I . . ."

"I know. But you can't go home behind this one, Wesley. I swear, I won't keep you past the right time."

"You can't keep me."

"Yes, I can. Because you owe me, like Pet owed you."

Wesley focused on the kid's face, seeing deep into his skull. "What're you saying?"

"Didn't the old man look you in the face when you sent him home?" the kid demanded.

"You know he did."

"Then you need to look me in the face before you go, too."

Saturday, 1:45 a.m. The Ford pulled up outside the red steel door. The kid sat behind the wheel with a 12-gauge Ithaca pump gun across his knees. He held a Ruger .44 Magnum in his right hand. The engine was running, but it was impossible to hear, even with an ear against the fender. Wesley climbed out of the passenger seat and walked quickly to the door. He pulled a clear plastic bag from under his coat and extracted a long, thin tube of putty-colored material. He applied the plastique evenly all around the door, between it and the frame; an extra blob with a string dangling from it went over the handle. Wesley pulled the string hard and moved quickly back across the street in the same motion.

The putty briefly sparked. There was a flash and a muted popping sound. The street was still empty. Wesley grabbed a large suitcase from the back seat, swung a duffel bag over his shoulder, and got out again.

The kid looked across at him. "Wesley, I'll have the radio tuned to pick up the TV station. I'll be in position a minute or so just before, okay?"

"I'll be coming out, kid."

"I know."

The Ford remained idling on the street until Wesley crossed and threw open the red steel door. He tossed his gear on the dark floor and closed the door from the inside, just as the kid crossed the street holding a gasoline-soaked rag. The kid wiped down the outside of the door as Wesley attached the floor-mounted brace from the inside. Working in unison even though they could no longer see each other, the kid and Wesley each broke open a full tube of Permabond and squeezed a beady trail of the liquid all around the edges of the door.

The kid smacked the door sharply twice with an open palm to tell Wesley that it looked fine from the outside now—in a few minutes, the door wouldn't open unless it was blasted again. The body language of the men he'd seen there before told Wesley that finishing this building wasn't a rush job, and a phone call had told him no work crew was scheduled for Saturday.

Wesley began to plan out his moves. Then he realized that his open hand was still pressed against the door in unconscious imitation of the way people said goodbye to each other in the Tombs—palms pressed against the cloudy Plexiglas.

The kid, driving the Ford back toward the Slip, was thinking, too. *He didn't take the dog with him.* That thought relaxed him, and he drove professionally the rest of the way.

Wesley worked carefully, slowly laying out the two dozen sticks of dynamite the kid had purchased from a construction worker a few weeks ago. After he had screwed in the blasting caps one at a time, he stuck them all together with more of the plastique putty, driving the wires through and around the deadly lump and into the rectangular transmitter. Finally, he gently positioned the unit under a dark-green canvas tarp in a far corner of the first floor.

Wesley climbed the seven flights of stairs to the top floor. The place was nearly completed. He found himself in a long hall, with doors opening into various rooms. He tried each room, looking across to the pier with the night glasses, making sure.

The elevator shafts were already finished, but no cars had been installed. There was another staircase at the opposite end of the building, parallel to the one Wesley had used.

Wesley stored all his stuff in the room he was going to use and began to retrace his steps. He tried the portable blowtorch on the steel steps first, but quit after a few minutes, only halfway through the first step. Then he pulled a giant can of silicon spray out of his duffel and began to spray each individual step carefully and fully, working his way up the steps backward until he again reached the top floor. Then he went down the parallel staircase to the first floor and worked his way back up again, repeating the procedure.

He looked down the stairs and gently tossed a penny onto the step nearest him. The penny slid off as if it were propelled and kept sliding all the way to the bottom of the flight. Satisfied, Wesley then applied the Permabond to each of the two top doors. He used all the remaining silicon to paint his way back toward the entrance of the room he was going to use.

He walked to the opposite end of the floor and worked his way backward, so that the only clear spot on the floor was in the very middle. Then he stepped inside the door and, without closing it, sprayed an extra-thick coat around the threshold. Finally, he closed the door and applied a coat of sealant to the inside.

It was 3:18 a.m. when he finished. Between Wesley and the ground floor were some incredibly slippery stairs, all separated by doors bonded to their frames.

Wesley set his tripod way back from the window, only about three feet from the door. No matter how the sun rose the next day, the shadows would extend at least this far back. Wesley would be shooting out of darkness, even at high noon. He went to the window and leaned out. The street below was narrow and empty. It was a long way to the ground.

Wesley took a long coil of 11mm black Perlon line from his duffel. It would support five thousand pounds to the inch. He anchored it securely to the window frame and tested it with all his strength. He laid the coiled line inside the window and attached the pair of U-bolts to the window frame to make sure.

Next, he spread a heavy quilt on the floor. On it he

placed a bolt-action Weatherby Magnum. From all Wesley's research, this one had the flattest trajectory, longest range, and greatest killing power. He'd tried several rifles set up for the NATO 5.56mm cartridge, but the Weatherby gave him the best one-shot odds. If he put one of the Nosler 180-grain slugs anywhere into Fat Boy, that would get it done.

He and the kid had talked it over for hours. The kid wanted Wesley to go for the chest shot, since it was a much bigger target. But Wesley had shown him the new LEAA newsletter with its successful field-tests of the new Kevlar weave for bulletproof fabric. The publication said the weave would turn a .38 Special at near point-blank range, and Wesley figured Fat Boy to be triple-wrapped in the new stuff.

The 2-24X zoom scope was bolted to the rifle's top; the whole piece was designed so that the bolt could be worked without disturbing the setting. He put the spotting scope, the windage meter, and a handful of cartridges down on the quilt. A silencer was out—there would only be the one chance, so accuracy ruled over all other considerations.

Wesley removed the deerskin gloves, and the surgeon's gloves he wore underneath. His palms were dry from the talc. Wesley took the auger with the four-inch bit and drilled sixteen precise holes in the room—in the walls and in the floor. Into each he put a stick of dynamite. The dynamite was connected with fusing material, and the whole network again connected to one of Pet's zinc-lined boxes. It would have been better to take all the stuff with him, but that would cost time he wouldn't have. Wesley taped the other eight sticks of dynamite together and wired them to the door, with a trip mechanism set against the chance the radio transmitter would fail to fire. If he had to remain in the room, sooner or later the cops would be breaking down the door.

It was 4:11 a.m. when Wesley finished this last task. None of the metal in the room gleamed—it had been worked with gunsmith's bluing and then carefully dulled with a soapy film. All the glass was non-glare, and Wesley was dressed in the outfit he had field-tested on the roof. He was invisible even to the occasional pigeon that flew past. Wesley hated the foul birds. He could hear Carmine's voice: *"I never saw a joint without pigeons; fucking rats with wings!"*

Wesley had no food with him, and no cigarettes, but he did have a canteen full of glucose and water, and he took a deep pull just before he went into a fix on the window. He came out of it, as he planned, at 6:30. The city was already awake. Staying toward the back of the room, he took the readings that he needed. The building was 118 feet high at window level; the pier was 1,750 feet from where he stood.

He stepped behind the tripod and refocused the scope. There was no ship at the pier, but he swept its full length and he knew he'd have a clear shot no matter where Fat Boy got off.

Wesley went toward the back of the room again, crossed his legs into a modified lotus, and sat focusing on the window ahead of him, mentally reviewing everything in the room and all the preparations inside.

The building outside the one room was blocked off completely. There was no way to go back downstairs. Wesley's entire mind was focused out the window. Mentally reviewing the picture of Fat Boy the kid had clipped from *Newsweek*, Wesley knew the target would wear a ton of medals on his fat chest. And be *obviously* treated like a god when he walked down the ramp to the pier.

The crowd started to assemble well before 10:00 a.m. At first it seemed like it wasn't going to be such a big event after all—maybe three hundred people total, half of them government agents.

But the crowd kept growing, and Wesley saw the white helmets of the TPF keeping people back. They were moving against demonstrators. With the spotting scope, it was easy to read the carefully lettered signs:

AMERICA DOES NOT WELCOME TYRANTS!
KILLER OF CHILDREN!
LIKE FATHER, LIKE SON!

They should be the ones up here in this fucking window, flashed through Wesley's mind. He carefully plucked that thought and tossed it into the garbage can of his brain—the part that already contained questions about his mother and the name of the first institution he had been committed to, when he was four years old.

By 11:15, the crowd was good-sized, but not unruly.

Traffic was backed up on the West Side Highway as people rubbernecked to see what was going on down at the pier. The pier, which could accommodate two ocean liners at the same time, was still empty.

At 11:45, the mayor arrived in a helicopter with three men who looked like politicians from the ground, but more like bodyguards through the scope.

At 12:05 p.m., the first tugs steamed in, towing the ship. The crowd let out a major cheer, drowning the voices of the demonstrators. Wesley trained the scope on the face of their leader, searching carefully for anything dangerous. But the man seemed too beside himself with rage to have planned anything that might get in the way.

At 12:35 p.m., the gangplank was lowered from the ship to the dock. An honor guard came first, flying the Haitian flag and the American flag in separate holders. The soldiers held their rifles like they were batons. As the TV crews trained their cameras toward the entrance to the gangplank, the reporters jockeyed for position at its foot.

At 12:42 p.m., Fat Boy started to walk down the gangplank. In what must have been a carefully orchestrated move, he stood alone, with bodyguards in front and behind, his white-clad body photogenically playing against the gangplank's fresh red paint.

Fat Boy halted. From the way the men behind him halted, too, the whole thing must have been rehearsed to death.

Fat Boy turned and waved to the crowd. A huge roar went up and surrounded him. Wesley felt a lightness inside him, one he had never felt before. A glow came up from his stomach and started to encircle his face. But it had too many years of breeding and training to compete with. Wesley went into total focus on the scope, seeing Fat Boy's face fill the round screen. He saw the crosshairs intersect on Fat Boy's left eye.

The crowd was now in a huge, rough semicircle around the base of the gangplank, and the noise was terrific. The wind held steady at seven miles per hour from the west—the tiny transistor-powered radio, which picked up only the Coast Guard weather reports, gave Wesley a bulletin every fifteen minutes. He had cranked in the right windage and elevation hours ago and stood ready to adjust. But everything had held static.

Wesley slowed his breathing, reaching for peace inside, counting his heartbeats.

Fat Boy turned to his left to throw a last wave at the crowd, just as Wesley's finger completed its slow backward trip. The sharp *cccrack!* came at a higher harmonic than the crowd noise. It seemed to pass over the crowd in a wave of sound as Fat Boy's head burst open like a rotten melon with a stick of dynamite inside.

Instantly, the screaming took on a higher pitch. His bodyguards rushed uselessly toward the fallen ruler as Wesley smoothly jacked a shell into the chamber and pumped another round into Fat Boy's exposed back, aiming this time for the spinal area. It seemed to him as if the shots echoed endlessly, but nobody looked in his direction. Still, it wouldn't take the TPF too long to figure things out.

Wesley stood up, stuck the two expended shells in his

side pocket out of habit, and ran to the window. Without looking down, he tossed the coil over the sill and followed it out. Wesley rappelled down with his back to the waterfront, both hands on the nylon line. Either the kid would cover him or he wouldn't—he didn't have any illusions about protecting himself with one hand holding on to the rope. The bottom of his eyesight picked up the Ford as he slid down the last twenty feet.

Wesley hit the ground hard, rolled over onto his side, and came up running for the back door, which was lying open. He grabbed the shotgun off the floor of the Ford, heard running footsteps, and saw the kid charging toward the car, holding a silenced, scoped rifle. The kid tossed the rifle into the back seat, and the Ford moved off like a soundless rocket, as smoothly as Pet ever could have done.

The quiet car worked itself lost in the narrow streets of the area. The kid hadn't said a word—he was watching the Halda Tripmaster clicking off hundredths of a mile. Just before the machine indicated .99, the kid slammed the knife switch home. A dull, booming sound followed in seconds, but the echoes reverberated for another full minute after the Ford had re-entered the West Side Highway and was passing the World Trade Center on the left.

The Ford sped back to the Slip without seeming to exceed the speed limit. A touch of the horn ring forced the garage door up, and the kid hit it again to bring it down almost in the same motion. The door slammed inches behind the Ford's rear bumper. Both men sprinted out from the Ford and jumped into the cab, which was out the door and heading for the highway again almost immediately.

Wesley inserted the tiny earplug and nodded to the kid, who turned on the police-band radio under the front seat. It was more static-free than the regular police units, and Wesley could hear everything clearly.

All units in vicinity Pier 40, proceed to area and deploy.

TPF is in charge. Acknowledge as you go in. Repeat: acknowledge as you go in.

Unknown number of men spotted in building directly across from pier. Eighth floor, fourth window from left. Shots fired.

Then:

Central . . . Central, this is 4-Bravo-21, K? We're going to try the rear door. Get us some cover, K?

Four-Bravo-21, 4-Bravo-21: Do not enter the building! Repeat: Do not enter the building. Backup is on the way. You are under the command of the TPF captain on the scene. Do not enter. Acknowledge.

Wesley slid back the protective partition between the seats and tapped the kid on the shoulder. "Slow it down, kid—they're not even at the building yet."

The kid slowed the cab to a crawl, although it still appeared to be keeping up with the traffic stream. Wesley stayed locked into the police-band. Minutes crawled slower than the cab.

All units now in position, acknowledge.

A series of *"10-4"*s followed as each car called in.

Central went back to a stabbing in Times Square. Wesley tapped the kid again; unobtrusively, the cab sped up.

The cab passed by the building on the highway very slowly; traffic was clotted as the drivers bent their necks to see what was happening. The pier was a single blotch of people and ambulances. The cab finally came to a dead stop in the traffic. From where they sat, they could see that the building was completely intact.

"I guess we got the window blown out in time," Wesley said. "They never noticed the rope hanging down."

"There *was* no rope hanging down—that's what I was doing with the piece while you ran into the car," the kid replied.

"You fucking *shot* the rope down?!"

"It wasn't hard—black line against a red building. I figured it would only cost us a second or so, and the rope hanging down was the only piece anyone could've photographed. Before, I mean."

"How many shots you have to fire?"

"I got it the first time—I cut loose as soon as you let go and dropped."

"You've got Pet's blood in you, kid. And better eyes than I ever had."

Wesley spotted a SWAT team deploying on the roof. He flicked the walkie-talkie to the intercept band.

Not a fucking sound in there, Sarge. Want us to go in?

Negative! Stay right there! Hostage Teams's getting on the horn down here first—maybe the bastards'll surrender.

The cop's short laugh barked over the speaker. Then the bullhorn's battery-powered voice blasted the air.

You men up there! This is Captain Berkowitz of the Tactical Patrol Force. Throw down your weapons and walk out of the back door one at a time, with your hands away from your bodies. You will not be harmed. The building is completely surrounded—there is no way you can leave. You have to surrender peacefully—don't make it any worse on yourselves.

It didn't surprise Wesley that only silence came out at the police from the building. The cop was back on the horn again.

Listen, you people . . . the man you shot isn't dead—he isn't going to die! This isn't a murder rap yet—don't make it one! Come out without your weapons or we're coming in. You have thirty seconds.

The kid said "Fuck!" softly, almost beyond audibility, but Wesley had been listening for it.

"He's dead, kid," Wesley told him. "The first shot took his face off. The cops are just running a hustle, that's all."

"They said . . ."

"Doesn't mean anything. We're not the only ones who don't play by the rules. Fat Boy is gone to heaven, I promise you."

One of the cops on the roof leaned far over, two more behind him, each holding one of his legs. The courageous cop lobbed in a tear-gas grenade; the wind carried the gas right out of the window of the sealed room, and it stayed quiet. Then a sharp *bang!* broke the silence.

"They must of figured they wasn't going to break in that street door," Wesley said.

While the TPF captain kept up a steady stream of threats and promises, the floor of the building rapidly filled with cautious policemen who started up the stairs. They slid back, cursing and frightened. Picking up their report, the captain tried the bullhorn again: *"All that crap on the stairs isn't going to keep us out forever, men! You've got nowhere to go! Make it easy on yourselves!"*

A break in traffic opened up, and the kid shot for it like any good city hackster. They followed the highway to 23rd Street and doubled back toward the building. Four blocks from the site, they found traffic choked off again—a burly street cop was gesturing threateningly at anyone who tried to get by.

The police-band was frantically screaming instructions to all units again. About thirty men had entered the building and were slowly making their way up the stairs with the aid of sandbags. . . . Then they were even more slowly taking down each door on their way to the top. It was 2:45 p.m.

The kid made a gross U-turn right in front of the burly cop, and the cab headed back toward Times Square. This time, they angled toward the water and finally pulled up on Twelfth Avenue just past 26th Street, right in front of the Starrett-Lehigh Building. The huge, abandoned terminal had a giant SPACE AVAILABLE sign on its façade.

"There's going to be a whole lot of motherfucking

space available in one building I know about," Wesley said. "Are we still within range?"

"Easy," the kid responded. "We got about four-tenths of a mile leeway."

"The building's about as full as it's going to get now. Hit the switch before they get into the room."

"What's the difference?"

"I set the dynamite to blow upward, you know? I just wanted to blow out that one room, so's they won't find anything. We need at least one body so they won't catch wise—it should look like the guys in that room decided to check out together instead of surrender."

The kid didn't reply. He reached forward and pushed the three buttons on the radio transmitter in correct sequence. In seconds, there was the familiar dull-booming throb, followed by a space-muffled crash. At their distance, it wasn't very impressive.

The cab turned right at 42nd and slowly threaded its way back east. They picked up the FDR Drive down by the river and headed back toward home.

As soon as they got inside their building, both men went to Wesley's apartment, after first setting all the security systems and leaving the dog in the garage. Wesley flicked on the television. The picture showed a milling mob that the police were trying to control, and not being too gentle about it. The TV announcer had a huge bulb-headed microphone with a white numeral "4" on its base. He looked harried.

"One of the worst tragedies in the history of our city—Prince Duquoi has been assassinated by person or persons unknown, and the killers have apparently blown up the building in which they were trapped in an effort to avoid capture. At least four police officers are missing in the wreckage and presumed dead. The fire department is on the scene, and rescue crews are working at top speed to clear the debris. The building from which the shots came is apparently owned by a major firm, but we have been unable to contact anyone at their office as of yet. . . ."

Wesley clicked off the set and looked at the kid. "Not dead, huh? That's what cops do, kid. Lie."

"I should've known," the kid said. "You think they'll find anything?"

"Not this year."

Wesley couldn't get any reliable info about Haiti on the radio or TV for days. The papers were mostly full of the destruction in the building across from the pier. The one thing that puzzled the police so far was the absence of any bodies that could have belonged to the killers—they continued to refer to the assassination as the work of several men.

Several cops privately told their reporter contacts that the killers had been blown into such small particles that the lab boys would never be able to identify anyone. The FBI was asked to enter the case. So as not to offend NYPD, the media were fed the presumption that the killers had crossed state lines in the preparation of the crime.

The CIA outbid the FBI and the locals—and promptly collected a ton of useless information. Wesley finally found what he was looking for in the *Times*.

Port au Prince, Haiti—The recent assassination of Prince Duquoi was apparently part of a military coup on this Caribbean island once ruled with an iron fist by Prince Duquoi as it was by his father before him, the infamous "Papa Du." A spokesman for the provisional military government announced that the island was completely under control and that Générale Jacques Treiste would temporarily assume command until free democratic elections could be held. If such elections follow the former pattern established by "President for Life" Duquoi, the island will undoubtedly remain a dictatorship.

It is not known how the islanders will react to the rule of a strictly military regime. "Papa Du" was widely believed to have occult powers stemming from his intimate relationship with the dark gods of obeah. His son, appointed following the old ruler's death, was actually controlled by Duquoi's wife. Any relationship between Générale Treiste and Mrs. Duquoi is unknown at this time, but insiders believe there will be no change.

Wesley read the article over several times, then slammed it to the floor in disgust. The dog jumped, startled—it had never seen Wesley move with such a violent lack of smoothness. Neither the dog nor Wesley left the room. The TV was never off; the radio would click on to an all-news station whenever the TV was muted.

The kid brought the papers every day. Four days later, Wesley found the confirmation he was expecting.

Port au Prince, Haiti—Earlier today, Madame Duquoi, the former wife of the infamous "Papa Du" Duquoi and mother of the recently assassinated Prince Duquoi, was married to Générale Jacques Treiste, head of the provisional military government of Haiti, in a lavish ceremony attended by numerous heads of state.

"I am in constant communication with my husband. This marriage is at his wish, so that the great nation of Haiti can continue to show the unity and strength that has marked its recent period of growth. My son died for his country, as did his father before him. In Président Treiste, we have a new leader . . . a leader who serves with the blessings of both my husband and my son."

Madame Duquoi, as she still prefers to be known, told journalists that her son knew there would be an assassination attempt if he came to America, and that a Communist plot to overthrow the government was behind the killing.

Inside sources also reported that a brief armed rebellion by guerrillas in the southern part of the island was crushed by 2,500 Haitian troops with-

out difficulty. Persistent rumors that American troops were involved have been denied.

Wesley stared at the newsprint until it blurred and faded. He focused on the white paper from which the black print was disappearing.

It was dark by the time he went down to the garage. The kid had the intake manifold and the heads off the Ford and was working under a single hanging trouble-light.

"It didn't work, kid."

"I know—I read it, too. Those niggers got no fucking guts."

"Forget that shit. It's not guts. All people got guts when it means enough to them. A woman once tried to take me out with a tiny little knife when I was holding a full-auto at her chest. Because of her kid, you know? I think there's gotta be *another* way the weasels do it, and I don't know what it is. Like in the joint, right? How come we got *any* informers in the joint? We should all be against the hacks, right? But they get your nose open. They make you think about yourself so much you don't ever think about yourself—you know what I mean?"

"Yeah. In the training school, they used to give you a parole if you grabbed a kid trying to run. The bigger guys used to make the little kids run, so's they could catch them."

"They make you run?" Wesley asked, curious.

"The first time I was in, they did. And they caught

me and beat me with that fucking strap until I couldn't stand. And *then* they threw me in the Hole for thirty days. The motherfucker who caught me got to go home."

"You didn't learn nothing from that?"

"The next time, as soon as I got out of the Hole, I went up to another big one and told him I wasn't getting my ass whipped for nothing. I told him I'd run again, but he had to leave me his radio when he went home. And I told him I wanted some money, too. He said okay—probably laughing himself to death—and I went over the fence the next damn night. I told him I'd meet him by the big tree just about a hundred yards outside the fence. I was waiting for him up in the branches. I dropped a big rock right on his skull and split it wide open. I thought he was dead, and I was going to hat up . . . but I could see him breathing, so I dragged him back to the fence and screamed up at the guards. They threw *him* in the Hole when he got out of the hospital, and *I* got to go home."

"That was good."

"Yeah. But I didn't *have* no home, so they put me in this foster home upstate. It was no different—they fucking beat you, and you worked all day on this fucking farm. They told me I'd have to stay until I was eighteen. I split from there, too. I was going to burn down the motherfucker's barn, but I didn't want to get a freak-jacket if they ever picked me up again."

"You learned a lot earlier than I did," Wesley told him. "Yeah, the only way we get to beat them even a little bit is to beat ourselves. It's like . . ."

Wesley pulled a soft pillow off the kid's cot and held it in front of him.

"Here. Punch this, as hard as you can."

The kid viciously slammed his fist into the pillow, deforming it but not tearing the cover.

"You see how it comes right back?" Wesley asked, fluffing it up. "You see how you can't hurt it no matter how hard you hit it? That's what their system is like, I think. . . . I think *now*, anyway."

"You can blow up a pillow."

"Not a real good one. They got one so soft and flexible that it *keeps* readjusting . . . but it fucking *stays* a pillow—like that Haiti bitch marrying that general. There's got to be another way, but I can't figure it. That's what you're here to do. Me, I'm here to clear the shit out of the way for you."

"This means you're going home?"

"No. Not now. There's still some of it I do understand. . . . Some more shit to clean up. When I go home, I'm going to leave you a clean piece of paper to draw on. You stay inside—from now on, I'm going out. And I'm going to look around. The next time I leave here with stuff, I won't be coming back. . . . Whole *mess* of motherfuckers won't be coming back, either.

"I know this: it's gonna be right here—no more of this overseas stuff. Right here, right in our own country."

"It's not our country."

"Then whose is it? If we can't have it, maybe nobody should have it."

"Nobody can blow up America, Wesley."

"Right. But I can sure as hell make them *think* somebody can."

The next morning, the Firebird slipped out of the garage and made its way up Water Street and then over to the FDR. Wesley followed the Drive to the 59th Street Bridge and crossed into Queens; he took Northern Boulevard through Long Island City, Woodside, and Jackson Heights, watching the neighborhoods change as he passed through.

He crossed Junction Boulevard and into Corona. By the time he reached 104th Street, it was as much a slum as anything Wesley had seen in Manhattan. A young black man, built like a weightlifter, with huge tattoos on his arms, crossed in front of Wesley's windshield. He glanced into the Firebird and caught Wesley's eye. *He's going to do the same thing as I am,* Wesley thought, but the black man's expression never changed.

Wesley crossed 114th, passed Shea Stadium, and followed the signs to the Whitestone Bridge. As the Firebird climbed over the bridge, Wesley saw LaGuardia Airport on his left. He threw two quarters into the exact-change basket and followed the signs to Route 95 North.

He saw the giant crypt they called Co-op City on his right and thought about dynamite. *It'd take a fucking nuclear attack,* he thought. Anyway, it was full of old people, and they couldn't breed anymore.

Wesley kept driving at a sedate fifty-five until he saw the signs for Exit 8. He turned off then; a right to North Avenue and then another right, driving through downtown New Rochelle. Moving aimlessly, guided by something he didn't understand but still trusted, Wesley drove past Iona College on his right and then turned right on Beechmont. He followed this up a hill surrounded by some lavish houses until he reached a long, narrow body of water.

This was Pinebrook Boulevard and Wesley noted the "No Thru Trucking" signs near the large thirty-miles-per-hour warnings. He followed Pinebrook until he reached Weaver Street. A furrier's truck passed him, doing at least forty-five. He turned left and followed the street to Wilmot Road, where he noted a pack of long-haired white kids with

SCARSDALE
ENVIRONMENTAL
CORPS

lettered on their T-shirts. They were aimlessly hanging around an open truck with a bunch of earth-working tools in its bed.

Wesley saw a light-green Dodge Polara police car, its discreet white lettering tastefully proclaiming its functions and duties. Wesley saw St. Pius X Church just ahead and turned left onto Mamaroneck Road. He drove steadily down this road until he saw a sprawling, ultra-modern structure on his left. He swung the car between the gates and motored slowly toward the entrance. The sign told Wesley all he needed to know: HOPEDALE HIGH SCHOOL.

The kids hardly glanced at the greaser-class Firebird. They sat on polished fenders of exotic cars, creatures from another planet to Wesley. But he didn't need that excuse. . . .

It took fifty-five minutes to get back into Manhattan and only another twenty to get into the garage. The kid was waiting for him.

"I went to your place to see if the dog wanted to go upstairs and run around," he said. "He wouldn't even let me in the door."

"I know—he's like me. This time, he *goes* with me, too."

"What do you need?" the kid asked.

"A refrigerator truck with some very professional lettering on the sides. I need a dual exhaust system on it, and flex-pipe connectors to reach from the back up into the box."

"Who's gonna be in the box?"

"They all are, this time. Now, listen to me; there's a lot more. I need a two-hundred-gallon tank with a high-speed inlet valve, and I need a mushroom of plastic explosive rigged from the roof . . . so everything in the truck explodes *down*, toward the ground, not up into the air.

"I need fifty hundred-pound bars of pure nickel, and I need around a couple dozen of those pressure bottles they keep helium in. Now, listen: *buy* this stuff if you can. If you got to steal it, leave anyone you find right there. This is the last time, and everything's got to be perfect."

"I'll get it all, Wesley."

"And find out when school opens each day at Hopedale High—it's a 914 area code—and class hours, if you can. The Westchester Library'll have a floor plan of the building, too."

It took the kid almost five weeks to assemble all the equipment. Inside the garage stood a huge white refrigerator truck with PASCAL'S FINEST ARGENTINA BEEF lettered in a flowery, blood-red script. The tank was installed inside. Wesley and the kid screwed off the top, laid it on its side on the floor of the truck, and carefully loaded in the nickel bars.

"Those assholes won't think there's something strange about a rich man ordering a whole lot of beef, stock his personal freezer," Wesley said. "This is what we do now, we extract the carbon monoxide and fill the tanks, then we—"

"Just from the truck's exhaust?"

"No. That crap is only seven percent carbon monoxide—we need pure stuff."

"I guess seven percent can snuff you all right," the kid said. "Like when those kids checked out together? In their car, last week?"

"Yeah, but it's not quick enough . . . and it don't work in the open air. When we play the pure stuff over those nickel bars inside a pressurized tank at exactly fifty degrees centigrade, we get perfect nickel carbonyl, okay? That's one million times as potent as cyanide. It'll work in open air, and it has an effective range of about five miles if there's no wind. But the explosion's got to be light—we don't want to blow this stuff way up in the air, and the extra heat would only screw things up."

"You want a *steady* fifty degrees centigrade, right?"

"Yeah," Wesley confirmed. "Can you get this truck to reach it and hold it there?"

"Sure. That's only about one hundred and twenty-two Fahrenheit—I looked it up. These rigs work both ways—they can heat as well as cool, no problem."

"Okay," Wesley said, "here's the deal. Under pressure, this gas'll set up in about ten minutes . . . enough to fill the big tank after the small tanks of carbon monoxide are emptied. I need the explosive so that when I blast it all open, it'll mushroom *low*. It gets too high, it won't do the job for us. This is a nice, heavy gas—it should stay low for a good while."

"How you know it'll work?"

"We're going to test it first. In one of the small tanks, with just a small piece of the nickel. We'll stuff it into this," he said, holding up the pressure tank for the miniature blowtorch. "You'll be with me on the test. And then that's all, right?"

The kid didn't answer—he was already at work, silently.

Two days later, the experiment was ready. The cab pulled out—Wesley driving, the kid in the back. The kid was dressed in chinos and a blue denim work shirt. A duffel bag sat next to him, ready for a shoulder-carry. In his pocket was a roll of bills totaling $725.

It was 11:15 p.m. when the cab pulled up past the corner of Dyer and 42nd. The kid stepped quickly out of the back seat and walked toward the Roxy Hotel.

He looked nervous as he approached the desk clerk, a gray, featureless man of about sixty. The kid pulled a night's rent from the big roll—the .45 was clumsily stuck into his belt, not completely covered by his tattered jacket. The clerk gave him a key with "405" on it; without saying a word, the kid turned to climb the stairs.

Wesley entered the hotel just as the kid disappeared up the stairs. He wore his night clothing, the soft felt hat firmly on his head. Under the hat was a flat-face gas mask of the latest Army-issue type. It had replaceable charcoal filters—inserted in the front opening, they could withstand anything but nerve gas for up to thirty-five minutes. It was held on top of Wesley's head by elastic straps and was invisible from the front.

Wesley approached the clerk, whose hand was already snaking toward the telephone.

"Remember me?" Wesley asked.

The clerk didn't know Wesley's face, but he knew what those words meant. He whirled for the phone again as Wesley slipped the gas mask into place and pressed the release valve on the miniature blowtorch. The greenish gas shot across the counter and into the clerk's face. He coughed just once as his face turned a sickly orange. The clerk slumped to the floor, his fingers still clawing for the phone. As he hit the ground, the kid came down the stairs with a gas mask on his face, carrying a Luger with a long tube silencer. He walked deliberately past Wesley, who had already stuffed the now exhausted gas cylinder into his side pocket and pulled out a pistol of his own.

The kid slipped the gas mask from his face as he

climbed into the front seat of the cab, the chauffeur's cap on his head; the flag dropped as Wesley hit the back seat.

The cab shot crosstown, toward the East River. The kid spoke quietly. "I had to waste one of the freaks upstairs—he came into my room with a knife before I could even close the door."

"You leave the room clean?"

"Perfect—I never got a chance to even sit down. Anyway, the charge in the duffel bag will go off in another few minutes."

"That clerk was gone before he hit the ground," Wesley said. "The stuff worked perfect."

"Was he the same one?"

"I couldn't tell for sure. But he was guilty, all right."

The cab whispered its way toward the Slip. It was garaged by midnight.

Thursday, 9:30 p.m. Wesley and the kid were completing the final work on the truck.

"Tomorrow there'll be a full house. The Friday assembly period's at eleven-thirty—there'll be almost four hundred kids in the joint."

"Wesley . . ."

"Yeah?"

"How come you're taking the gas mask?"

"I'm not going out that way, kid. The gas's for *them*, right? I won't leave them a fucking square inch of flesh to put under their microscopes—no way they're coming back here to look for you. You're going to keep this place, right?"

"I don't know," the kid said. "I guess so. But I'm going to find a couple other places, too . . . and fix them."

"Good. And be *out* there, right? Everything you learn, teach—there's a lot of men out there who'd listen, and you know how to talk to them."

"Women, too."

"They already know, kid. You see how the pillow snapped back into place in Haiti? It was a woman who held it. She must've of been the one behind the old man, and the kid, too."

"Maybe . . . It don't matter anyway—I'll know who to talk to."

"You got to be different from the way we were, kid. We never had no partners, except in blood. I never could figure out how all those black guys run around calling each other 'brother'—the most that could mean is that the same womb spilled you, and even *that* don't mean a thing.

"You're not going to be alone, kid. You know why? 'Cause if you are you end up like me. Carmine thought he built a bomb, but he didn't. I'm a laser, I think. I can focus so good I can slice anything that gets in the way. But I can't see nothing between me and the target. When I was in Korea, I thought I'd be the gun and they'd point me. But that didn't make no sense, even then. So it don't make sense to have any of the other scumbags point me, either. . . ."

"What other scumbags?"

"Like those Weathermen or whatever they call themselves. Writing letters to the fucking papers about which building they're going to blow up . . . or blowing themselves up instead. Bullshit. But I know how they feel—they got nothing of their own to fight for, so they made something up. The blacks don't want them; the Latinos don't want them; the fucking 'working class,' whatever that is, don't want them. . . . And they don't want themselves."

"Why didn't the blacks want them?"

"Want them for what? All those nice-talking creeps want is to be generals—the niggers're supposed to be their fucking 'troops.' The blacks can see *that* much, anyway."

"I've talked to a few of them—the revolutionaries. But I can't understand what the fuck they're talking about."

"Nobody can but themselves—and that's who they should stick to. It's like a fucking whore everyone in the neighborhood gangbangs, right? You might get yourself some of that, but you're damn sure not going to bring her home to meet your people."

"Yeah? *I* would, if—"

"—if you *had* people. But I get it—you're not like them. That's what their asshole 'system' is like—good enough to fuck around with, but not good enough to bring home, you understand?"

"Yeah. I guess I did even while they were still talking."

"They're out there, kid. Driving cabs, working in the mills, mugging, robbing, fighting, tricking . . . in the

Army. Anyplace they think they fit. There's a lot more of *us* than there are of *them*, but we don't know how to find each other. You got to do that—that part's for you."

"Why me?"

"Carmine had two names, right? Carmine Trentoni. And Pet had one and a half . . . *Mr.* Petraglia. How many names I got?"

"One. 'Wesley' is all I know."

"And how many you got, kid? What did we call you?"

"I see. . . ."

"But *they* won't. I *got* another name someplace—I had one in the Army, and I had one in the joint, and I had one that the State gave me until I really didn't have one no more. You ever see a giant roach?"

"No. Wesley, what're you—?"

"One time, Carmine and me decided to kill all the fucking roaches on our tier. We made this poison, right? It was deadly, had them all belly-up in a week. But after a few more weeks, we saw all kinds of strange roaches around. Some were colored almost white. And then we saw this giant sonofabitch—he musta been six inches long. And fat."

"That was one of those Florida things, Wesley. I read—"

"The fuck it was. I seen too many roaches to go for that—it was a goddamn mutant roach. They breed much faster than humans, and they *evolved* a special roach. One that *ate* the fucking poison, you see?"

"No."

"That giant roach would've died if Carmine and me

hadn't fed him, kid. All he could live on was the poison, and we didn't have too much left. When we ran out of the stuff, he just died."

"How is that like your name?"

"I'm like that giant roach. I can only live on the poison they usually use to kill us off . . . or make us kill each other off. That's why I'm going home tomorrow. But that poison can't kill you—you don't need it to live on, so you'll be a ghost. The ghost who haunts them all."

"How'm I going to find the answers?"

"I don't know. I *do* know they're not all in books. And don't be just listening to all kinds of silly motherfuckers. *Test* them all. You got enough money to hole up fifty years if you have to, right?"

"Yeah. How'm I going to bury you, Wesley? I don't want the—"

"The State birthed me—the fucking State can bury me, kid. Just watch the TV real close tomorrow. You'll see me wave goodbye."

They both went back into Wesley's apartment. After Wesley told the dog to stay put, he showed the kid all the systems, where everything was. It took several hours. Then Wesley stood up and stretched.

"I'm going up on the roof, kid. Get everything ready—I'll be pulling out around ten tomorrow."

Wesley smoked two packs of cigarettes on the roof, thinking. The *News* only reported the "heart attack" death of the desk clerk because it was in the same hotel where a half-nude man was found shot to death—a bullet in his chest, one in his eye, and another in the back of his neck. A low-yield explosion had blown out most of the floor.

He thought of calling Carmine's widow to tell her about the fifty thousand in the basement, but decided to tell the kid about it instead.

Wesley spotted a tiny fire out on the Slip—it was getting cold again, and the tramps would have to make their usual arrangements. Wesley realized that he wasn't sleepy.

And that he'd never sleep again.

By 10:30 the next morning, everything was ready. The dog sat on its haunches in the corner of the garage. When Wesley snapped his fingers, it ran forward and leaped into the truck's cab. Wesley started the engine; it rumbled menacingly in the sealed garage.

He looked down at the kid, who was looking up.

"How old're you, kid?"

"Twenty-six, I think."

"I don't want to see you for a lot of years, right?"

"I'll be here, Wes."

"You got your own brain, but you're my blood. All my debts are canceled—the only reason you're out here now is for yourself, right?"

"For all of us."

"If something fucks up, I'll get across the bridge before I let go. You know what to do if they come here?"

"I always knew that."

Wesley pressed his hand against the window glass, palm out—the kid's palm flattened against his.

The kid turned and hit the garage button. Wesley released the clutch, and the big truck rumbled out onto Water Street. As they headed for the bridge, Wesley spoke to the dog. "Keep your fucking head down. As ugly as you are, they'd see something was wrong for sure."

The dog sat on the floor of the cab, on the other side of the gearshift lever. The thermometer on the dashboard, calibrated in centigrade, read a steady fifty degrees, the speedometer an equally steady forty-five.

Since he was wheeling a truck, Wesley remembered not to take the exact-change lane. He paid the White-stone toll and motored sedately onto 95 North. The big truck moved through New Rochelle without drawing a glance—it wasn't the only rig on North Avenue.

It was almost 11:10 when Wesley turned onto Pine-brook Boulevard, just as a squad car passed. By 11:15, he was turning into the school parking lot.

Wesley drove the truck right up to the front entrance of the stone building. He got out quickly and threw a series of switches. The carbon monoxide hissed into the giant tank loaded with the nickel bars; a heavy-voltage current shot through all the hardware holding the truck doors closed, also priming the system to release the explosive with that same move.

Wesley drew a couple of curious glances, but nobody said a word. He opened the cab of the truck and snapped his fingers for the dog to jump down. Then he pulled two large suitcases and a heavy canvas duffel bag from the cab.

He reached back inside and pulled what looked like the choke cable. A tiny, diamond-tipped needle slammed into the plastic distributor cap, and five cc's of sulfuric acid ran into the points; nobody could hope to start the truck now, even with a key. A quick twist on the valve of each tire sent a similar needle slamming home, and the tires started to drain—the slow hiss was audible only if you stood very close.

Wesley shouldered the duffel bag, grabbed a suitcase in each hand, and walked up the flower-bordered concrete path to the main door, the dog trotting along behind him as silent as a fish in deep water. Students and teachers looked at him curiously, but the elderly lady didn't seem surprised when Wesley stopped in front of her. "Pardon me, ma'am. Could you direct me to the auditorium?"

"Certainly, young man. It's just down the end of this corridor." She gestured with a ringless left hand. "You'll see the signs."

"Thank you, ma'am."

Wesley turned and began to walk down the corridor. A teacher who looked like a college kid, with long brownish hair, a red shirt, and a silly, authoritative face stopped him. "Can I help you?"

"The auditorium," Wesley replied. "Gotta go fix the lights."

The young man looked at Wesley critically, but finally shrugged. "It's straight ahead," he said, and went back to his dreams of a marijuana paradise where all men were brothers.

Wesley found the auditorium. It had three doors across the back and an entrance on each side—five in all, too many to cover. The floor plan had been accurate.

The big room was empty. Wesley walked down the center aisle to the front row. He threw his equipment up on the stage and opened the duffel bag. He pulled out a pair of holsters and cartridge belts and strapped them on, sticking an S&W .38 Special with a four-inch barrel in one, the silenced Beretta in the other. He calmly took out the grease gun and bolted in the clip. The stopwatch on his wrist told him four minutes had elapsed—ten minutes to go to be on the safe side.

Wesley pushed all the equipment toward the back of the stage and tested the PA system to be sure it was working. He climbed off the stage, and had started to walk back up the aisle when the young teacher with the long hair came running down the aisle toward him.

"Hey, you! I just called Con Edison and they said there wasn't any—"

Wesley's first shot with the Beretta caught the young man in the chest, knocking him over two rows of seats. There was no reaction to the muffled sound.

Wesley kept walking unhurriedly toward the rear auditorium doors. The sealant went all around the openings of two doors, leaving the middle one open.

Wesley checked his watch—no more time. He snapped his fingers, and the dog rose from where he had been resting. Wesley pointed toward the left-hand side door and said "Watch!" The dog trotted into position. Then

Wesley quickly bonded the door and switched positions with the dog again, finishing the other one.

Leaving the dog lying down near the center of the stage, Wesley walked through the middle door, toward the signs that said ADMINISTRATIVE OFFICES.

The walls were all glass, floor-to-ceiling. Students were hanging over the long counter, asking questions about clubs and transcripts and bickering over their schedules, when Wesley walked in and swept the entire field with a long, screaming burst from the grease gun. In seconds, the whole room was red and yellow with human death. Wesley walked quickly around the counter and into the big office marked PRINCIPAL. A nice-looking woman, apparently the man's secretary, was seated at a kidney-shaped desk with her mouth wide open. No sound was coming out. Wesley shot her in the stomach with the unsilenced piece and kept walking.

A chubby man was in the office, crouched down behind a desk. A solid-looking older woman was frantically speaking into a phone. "Florence! Florence, get the police! Florence . . . ?"

Wesley walked in, and they both fell silent. Wesley looked at the man. "You the principal?"

The lady stood up to her full five-foot height. "*I'm* the principal."

She didn't look frightened. *Good,* Wesley thought, *maybe she'll do what she has to do.* "Get on the PA system and tell everyone to get into the auditorium," Wesley snapped at her. "Tell them there's been an emergency and to get a move on—"

"I won't do any such thing! Those children are in my—"

Wesley ripped her open with a short burst from the grease gun, thinking, *Fucking women and children—I should've known.* He spun the gun's barrel into the face of the crouching man. "*You* do it. Do it *fast!*"

The man's fingers were wet and trembly as he pushed the button for the PA system, but he couldn't make himself talk—only spittle came out. Wesley shot him with the revolver and grabbed the microphone.

"*Attention, please!*" He heard his voice echoing and knew the man must have turned it on correctly. "*There has been an emergency. All students and teachers proceed at once to the auditorium. Enter only by the middle door from the back. Repeat: This is an emergency—there is a bomb inside this building! Proceed to the auditorium at once!*"

He stepped out into the corridor just as he heard the police sirens in the distance. His watch said six minutes still to go before the gas was certain to be ready. Wesley stepped over the bodies in the outer office and sprinted back toward the auditorium. The frightened students seemed comforted by the sight of the man in military gear, obviously armed for their protection. They were already milling into the auditorium as Wesley rushed into the side door, smashing a pathway with the butt of the pistol. The dog was patrolling in front, keeping the students away from the stage.

Wesley ran to the dog. He turned to see a mob of terrified students streaming in through the middle door.

A tall cop was trying to shove his way through to the front. Wesley waited until the cop almost got through, and shot him in the face with the unsilenced pistol. He dropped the pistol and snapped a fresh clip into the grease gun.

The screaming got worse. The auditorium was nearly full of students and teachers, with all the others trying desperately to get inside—to safety.

Wesley aimed the grease gun at the middle door and screamed, "Get the fuck away from that door!" and cut loose with another burst before he switched clips again. Bodies went flying out into the hall, and the screams from the kids already inside made it impossible to hear anything else.

Wesley charged the one open door. The dog followed. Wesley used the grease gun to clear out what was left of the remaining people, jacked in his last clip, and ran forward. He managed to slam the door even against the frightened tide—they fell back when they saw Wesley . . . and the gun.

The dog went berserk, mouth foaming, snapping, keeping the remaining crowd away from Wesley. Students ran to the side doors, now trying to get out, only to find it was useless. The Permabond went around the middle door in seconds. Wesley turned and ran back toward the stage. He leaped up and grabbed the microphone with one hand, firing another burst into the ceiling. *"Shut the fuck up! Keep quiet or I start blasting again!"* The place quickly silenced, except for occasional whimpers. One kid was crying and couldn't stop. Wesley looked out at the horrified crowd, the grease gun still threatening the room.

"Stay quiet! The next one who screams gets killed!" He could hear the sirens clearly now—cops must be all over the place. His watch said it was still three minutes until the gas would be ready. Wesley's eyes swept the auditorium. He stopped at a husky-looking kid in a letterman's sweater. The kid caught Wesley's eye, too, and tried to look away.

"You! Come up here! Quick!"

The kid slowly climbed up out of his fear and walked quickly toward the stage. Wesley held the gun at the boy's face. He spoke without the microphone. "Climb up to that ledge by the side and go out a window. Tell the cops that I got me a few hundred hostages. Tell them I got enough dynamite in those suitcases over there to level this whole fucking school. Tell them I want to talk. You got that?"

"The windows don't open," the kid quavered "I—"

"*Break* the fucking windows! Move!"

The boy ran toward the side of the auditorium, causing a momentary stir. Wesley grabbed the microphone again—"Stay still! He's going out to get help for you!"—and they quieted. The kid finally clawed his way out of the window and dropped to the ground. Wesley's watch showed one minute still to go when he heard a familiar, bullhorned voice.

"You inside! What do you want? You can't get out!"

Wesley grabbed the microphone. The volume was already boosted as much as it could go, and he shouted at the top of his voice.

"I want a helicopter to take me to the airport, and I want a motherfucking 747 to take me to Cuba! You got that, pigs?"

Wesley figured that sounded sufficiently like the usual revolutionary bullshit to hold the cops for the minute or so he needed. The cop's voice came back immediately.

"Let the kids go! Let the kids go and we'll get you a plane!"

Wesley didn't answer. He flicked the switch on the transistor radio in his buttoned shirt pocket, and the tiny earplug gave him the public version. The announcer said that three units of the State Police as well as squads from New Rochelle, Larchmont, White Plains, and Scarsdale were all around a school building where an unknown group was holding hundreds of children hostage. The people inside had demanded a plane to Cuba but, remarkably, they hadn't mentioned a thing about ransom to release the hostages. . . .

Forgot the fucking ransom, Wesley thought, hoping his act wouldn't appear too bogus. If they knew . . . ? But his watch told him the time was up and he relaxed.

The loudspeaker outside crackled again.

"You inside! We've got the plane for you! Let all the hostages go and we'll send in some cops to replace them. Unarmed, okay?"

"How many cops you got out there?"

"Too many for you, punk!"

"Bring some more, motherfuckers!"

The bullhorn was silent—they must have been working over the lame asshole who had screamed that crap about "too many." A thing like that could make a man act crazy.

When the radio told him that the TV crews were in place outside, Wesley checked his watch again—12:03.

He slipped the gas mask over his face and sprayed the auditorium with one final blast from the grease gun. He pulled out a stick of dynamite, then immediately rejected it in favor of six similar sticks all taped together with a long fuse.

Everyone was screaming and crying and dying in the place. Wesley lighted the single stick and threw it with all his strength toward the rear of the auditorium. . . . It blew out half the wall, taking dozens of kids with it. Wesley bolted for the giant hole the explosion made, and the dog followed. They almost ran right into four cops stationed in the corridor. The dog covered the distance to them in a flash-second and was ripping at the first one's throat as Wesley spray-blanketed the corridor with bullets. As he leaped over the bodies, he saw the dog was hit along the spine. The animal was working hard to breathe—he didn't have long.

Wesley scooped up the dog in his arms and headed for the metal stairs leading to the roof. He gained the roof in seconds, and stepped out in clear view. He checked quickly: the screaming about the dynamite should have been enough to keep cops off the roof, but . . .

The roof was empty.

The TV cameras all focused on the single figure of a madman cradling a dog in his arms. Before anyone could shoot, or even react, Wesley knelt, gently lowered the dog to the roof, and pressed a transmitter button. The bottom and sides of the truck shot outward. A huge, dense cloud of greenish gas started to billow out over the ground. The explosion was still echoing while everyone ran for cover.

The kid was magneted to the TV in Wesley's apartment, watching and listening to the announcer.

"The unknown man on the roof has apparently detonated some sort of explosion on the ground. A squad of policemen has gone around the back to try and gain access to the roof. The darkness you see on your screen isn't your picture: apparently, some type of gas has been released from the truck. We're back about five hundred yards from the scene, so there shouldn't be any problem bringing the rest of this to you. . . . Wait! The man is lighting something! It looks like a torch! He's holding it high above his head. . . . He . . . Oh my God, he looks like the Statue of Liberty! He's . . ."

As the kid watched, the explosion darkened the picture screen and the announcer's voice faded away.

• • •

CHOICE OF EVIL

When his girlfriend, Crystal Beth, is gunned down at a gay rights rally in Central Park, Burke, the underground man-for-hire and expert hunter of predators, vows vengeance. But someone beats him to the task: a shadowy killer who calls himself Homo Erectus and who seems determined to wipe gay bashers from the face of the earth. As the killer's body count rises, most citizens are horrified, but a few see him as a hero, and they hire Burke to track him down . . . and help him escape. Burke is forced to confront his most harrowing challenge: the mind of an obsessive serial killer. And soon the emotionally void method behind the killer's madness becomes terrifyingly familiar, reminding Burke of his childhood partner, Wesley, the ice-man assassin who never missed, even when the target was himself. Has Wesley come back from the dead? The whisper-stream says so. And the truth may just challenge Burke's very sense of reality.

Crime Fiction

DEAD AND GONE

Career criminal Burke's skill at working the feather edges of the law are legendary, and this isn't the first time he's been hired to trade cash for an abducted kid. But when the meet turns out to be an ambush, Burke's partner is killed and he's left for dead. Dumped on the steps of the ER, Burke hovers between life and death. Meanwhile, the police—and whoever wants him dead—are circling closer, biding their time. Burke escapes the hospital, his face forever changed by the surgery that saved his life. The whisper-stream mutters that he's dead, and he is certainly gone. From New York, anyway. Burke is on the hunt, knowing he has to find whoever wanted him dead to protect his own life. And avenge his partner. Unable to call his own family for assistance, Burke goes into his past for help. All the way back to his origins as a "child of the secret." The trail starts in Chicago, continues into the Pacific Northwest, then to the remote mountains of New Mexico. And ends in a place that exists only in the dreams of the darkest degenerates on earth.

Crime Fiction

EVERYBODY PAYS

A hit man defies the confines of a life sentence to avenge his sister's batterer. An immaculately dressed man hires a street gang to extract his daughter from a Central American prison, for reasons as mysterious as they are deadly. A two-bit graffiti artist with a taste for Nazi-ganda finds himself face-to-face with three punks out to make a mark of their own—literally—with a tattoo needle. *Everybody Pays* contains 38 white-knuckle rides into a netherworld of pederasts and prostitutes, stick-up kids and fall guys—where private codes of crime and punishment pulsate beneath a surface system of law and order, and our moral compass spins frighteningly out of control. Ingenious plot twists transform the double-cross into an expression of retribution, the dark deed into a thing of beauty.

Short Stories/Fiction

VINTAGE CRIME/BLACK LIZARD
Available wherever books are sold.
www.weeklylizard.com